Why Didn't You Save Me?

WHY DIDN'T YOU SAVE ME?

(A story of Love, Patience, Healing, and Second Chances)

Tarina-Michelle

A Novel

This is a work of fiction. Names, characters, places, and incidents are either products of the author's imagination or used fictitiously.

ISBN: (979-8-234-03251-5)

Printed in the United States of America.

Dedicated to my siblings,

Many might be surprised by who I chose to dedicate this book to, but the truth is simple. A sibling becomes your first best friend.

Being the second oldest came with a great responsibility that I felt and honored deeply. I always wanted to be someone you could look up to, someone who set an example and protected you along the way. As I have grown older, that desire continues to grow.

Watching you guys look up to me over the years made me realize my value in ways I did not always see for myself. I believed I was your protector, but truthfully your belief in me protected me.

Your love, your trust, and the way you believed in me helped shape the person I am today.

This book is for you…. This book is for us!

Otis, Caprisha, Esela, Lela, Kawana, Chevone, Corey, and Arnay.

I love you all more than words will ever express.

CONTENTS

INTRO

Elisa jumped up from her sleep, drenched in a puddle of sweat, almost hyperventilating as the same dream replayed once again.

In this repetitive nightmare, Sampson was always there, reaching his hand out to save her from the chaos she did not realize that she had created.

She allowed herself to believe moving on was the right thing to do, after all, she never believed he truly wanted her fully.

Yet, even as life continued to move on, he lingered in her mind, and daily she was unable to shake him or the peace that she felt with him.

These dreams felt like punishment, a cruel reminder of what she had lost, or better yet what she pushed away.

All she wanted was for it to end, for Sampson to save her from the cold and dark place she was fighting internally like she dreamed and fantasize he would.

In her eyes, he could do nothing wrong.

He was the strongest man she had known aside from her dad.

And since her dad passed he was the only man who ever made her feel completely safe, mentally, emotionally, spiritually, and physically.

He had always shown up as a protector, provider, and a leader.

Even in the most uncomfortable moments, conversations, or situations, he would always see her as Elisa.

That's one of the many reasons that she loved and craved Sampson the way she did.

He had been her safe place, her place of peace, a place that no one else could access or cause her any harm.

But now as she sat on her bed hugging her pillow that was now soaked in tears, the one question that returned to her over and over, the words that stalked her more than the dream could ever do:

Why Didn't You Save Me?

Why Didn't You Save Me?

Chapter 1

He's Better Off Without Me

Elisa swung her legs over the side of the bed, her bare feet tipping against the cold hardwood floor. She shook her head, trying to remove the thoughts and weight of the dream she had last night.

She glanced at her clock on the nightstand. It was 3:25 AM.

Another night that she was unable to sleep through the night.

She sat at the end of the side of the bed staring out of the window. The city lights seemed fuzzy and gray. It was as if the weight and heaviness she was carrying was being reflected.

Her gaze had now drifted to the Bible on her nightstand, a gift from her grandmother years ago. Its leather cover was worn; the wording had faded over time.

She hadn't opened it in months.

Who was she kidding?

It was longer than that.

The feeling she had tonight was different. It was as if something was calling her to open it.

Her hands were shaky as she reached for the Bible. She did not know where to turn or what chapter to read, but she remembered her old pastor telling her that the book of Psalms was her prayer book.

She flipped through the pages of Psalms until she found a verse that was familiar:

"The Lord is close to the brokenhearted and saves those who are crushed in spirit."
(Psalm 34:18)

Crushed in spirit.

That was her.

The words felt like they were written for this very moment of her life.

Tears filled her eyes, spilling over as the dream kept replaying in her head.

Her home was so quiet all she heard was the vibration coming from the refrigerator in the kitchen.

The place, humongous, felt empty.

It felt sad, as if the place too grieved the absence of Sampson.

That Bible verse had her fuming mad, as it reminded her of how crushed in spirit she truly was.

Her eyes drifted to the box at her closet door.

It was all of Sampson's things, what was left of their time together. She never really planned on returning them to him, yet she packed them up to help her move on.

Inside the box were reminders of the love she was trying to forget yet failing miserably at doing so.

She opened the box to find her favorite hoodie of his, all of the handwritten notes he had written her.

She decided to open one of the written notes which said:

"I pray for your light daily… Never let it go out! You are necessary and I will always root for you to keep winning."

Tears still streaming as she remembered why he wrote her that note.

She was doubting herself in her career and he always knew the words to encourage her.

She closed her eyes while the haunting dream continued to play.

The pain felt fresh.

The hurt still felt fresh.

In her dream Sampson was not the same man she knew who commanded attention when he walked in any room.

Instead, he was anxious, almost to the point of despair, trying to save her, but there was something blocking him.

But from what?

Was he trying to save Elisa from herself, or from the lie she told?

Did he know that she really did not mean the words she uttered, "Sampson, I do not love you anymore"?

Truth be told, Elisa walked away because she thought it was the best thing for her to do.

Sampson deserved someone better than her.

He did not deserve the brokenness of Elisa.

She did what she thought would be best, but it caused her to lose part of herself and most definitely a shattered heart.

Why did she do this?

Why had she pushed her soulmate, her peace, and her comfort away?

Still sitting stuck with tears flowing, Elisa began to get upset, not with Sampson but with herself.

Reality was that she knew without a doubt that Sampson loved her with his entire heart, but there was still a little tinge deep down that would not allow her to fully believe it.

It was almost as if she had convinced herself that Sampson was simply too good to be true.

Why would a man this perfect want her?

And that she would never be able to hold on to him, especially once he saw the true Elisa unmasked.

It had been 7 months and six days and the memory of that night was still haunting her as if it was yesterday.

She could see his face.

His eyes trying to understand.

His heart pleading.

And his confident voice in that moment was so broken as he struggled to know what had changed.
As Elisa was walking away, Sampson brokenly screamed,

"Elisa, tell me you don't love me. Look me in my eyes and tell me you don't love me."

And in that moment, she lied and uttered the words,

"I do not love you anymore, Sampson!"

To her she was letting him go to find something whole.

She knew she had caused him pain.

She knew his pain was real and she wanted to hug him and reassure him, but she too had to live with those words, so she decided to walk away.

As she walked away, she did not look back.

And there Sampson was in the same spot, caught off guard and lost in his tears.

Though she walked away Elisa loved that man more than she could dare to admit or even put into words.

As she sat in her lonely and quiet home she had to face the consequences of her decision.

A decision that has her broken into pieces.

Her pain in that moment was unbearable and there was
nothing she could do about it but own it.

Own not only the pain but the emptiness she felt
without him.

Own the pain she caused him.

And own the pain that she would now have to live with.

Chapter 2

The Haunting Dreams

She tried to suppress the tears, but here she was sobbing like her life was about to end. There was no use in holding in the emotions, she thought, as she let out a heart-wrenching cry that came from all of the regret, the love, and the reality of what she had lost. She literally cried until she could no longer cry and was overcome with exhaustion from crying.

She drug herself to her bed, hugged her pillow as if it was Sampson, and whispered his name before she fell into a deep sleep.

Even as she rested, she was restless, because there was no escape.

Sampson followed her in her dreams.

Elisa felt like God was punishing her because why else would she dream of this man night after night?

Her dreams were always so clear and vivid. From his scent to his words, she felt everything. It was almost as if she could literally feel his touch.

And every time she would awake her heart grew wearier, and her heart felt more broken.

Everything reminded her of him.

Even her sleep did not allow her to retreat. The memories were too strong and present.

She could not forget them if she wanted to.

It was as if God was making her deal with her feelings, her emotions, her heart, even though she tried so hard to run from them.

Why wouldn't He just let her forget?

Why wouldn't He take these painful dreams away?

Why wouldn't He give her peace?

Why was God punishing her?

The morning was upon her, and Elisa was frazzled, tired, and empty from a repeated sleepless night.

The only thing that was on her side was she did not have to go into the office as it was Saturday morning.

She decided she would take the day to try to reset.

Running was always a way that helped clear her mind, so Elisa got dressed and made her way to the gym in her loft.

As she ran it was as if she finally had peace.

She was able to just focus on her feet hitting the treadmill in perfect rhythm and the music blaring in her headphones.

She started with a slow pace.

Then she increased the speed, pushing herself harder and harder.

In that moment she didn't think of Sampson.

Her mind was finally quiet.

She decided to run until her body said no more.

For the first time her thoughts of Sampson stopped suffocating her.

She had been running for 45 minutes, and the moment she stepped off that treadmill thoughts of Sampson were still there.

She could see his eyes and how he looked at her with such passion.

She could hear his voice and how he said her name.

She closed her eyes, and, in that moment, she could feel his embrace, the hugs he would give her that would lift her off her feet literally.

She realized she could not outrun her love for him.

How she was handling this breakup was unhealthy, and Elisa recognized that.

She couldn't let go.

She couldn't move on.

She couldn't stop thinking of him no matter how much time had passed.

No matter how hard she tried to forget she could not.

Running had become second nature as that was the only way she would find temporary refuge.

But the moment she stopped it was the same aching, the same hurt and pain because she loved him and nothing could change that.

For some reason the dreams of last night and the feeling in her stomach felt different.

Sampson was always on her mind, but it was different.

God, what is this she asked?

Is he ok?

Her pain shifted to worry, a worry that made her nauseous.

But the thought of picking up the phone to call him terrified her.

As calling was out of the question, Elisa decided to do something she said she would never do.

She went to his social media page.

As she began to type in his name her heart was racing like it was ready to pop out of her chest.

So many thoughts clouded her mind.

All of the what if scenarios played in her mind.

She swallowed as she hit enter.

The sound echoed through the room.

As his profile loaded there was a post from less than five minutes ago.

That gave her the relief she needed to know that he was ok.

The post said, "Thank you God for this new season of blessings."

He was surrounded by a group of runners.

Her stomach again fell ill as she recalled how running used to be something they did together.

She hated running before Sampson.

Though she used to run to stay in shape, Sampson helped her make running fun and less of a chore.

They used to laugh and encourage each other.

She didn't realize how seeing him moving on with life would hurt her.

She was grateful he was ok, but the pain of letting him go hit her like a ton of bricks.

She missed him so much and she had no one to blame but herself.

"What have I done?" she yelled at the screen as she stared at his picture.

As Elisa was getting ready for her shower she was stopped in her tracks at her reflection in the bathroom mirror.

She couldn't believe the visual of the woman looking back at her.

She looked worn, exhausted, and defeated.

Who is this, she said quietly to the image looking back at her.

She stood there in silence almost wishing she would get a reply.

The silence continued.

There was no reply.

Suddenly she said, Elisa, you have to get yourself together.

You need to find and be reminded of who Elisa is.

You now have to find a way to live with your decision.

It is time to get it together; she yelled at herself through the mirror.

After a large sigh she shook her head and stood up straight.

This evening is about fun times with her Sorors.

There was no time or need to wallow in self-pity.

It was a time to find herself again, to let her hair down, to feel beautiful and light again.

She made a pact with herself.

Today would not be a day of regrets.

It would not be a day of sadness and moping.

In addition, she definitely did not want everyone to ask a million questions either, an if she did not pull it together that would be the gist of their night.

When she stepped into the shower it was as if the hot water put her at instant ease.

Almost like she felt renewal.

As she put on her makeup she felt pretty, alive.

For once she felt like herself again.

She had purchased a dress specifically for this occasion.

It was a straight form fitting dress, simple yet hugging her curves in all the right ways, paired with skinny strappy heels.

That same reflection in her mirror she saw before her shower now felt beautiful, even sexy.

She promised that today she would leave all of the dead weight of her decisions behind and enjoy her night.

She owed it to herself.

Elisa got her sexy back as she grabbed her bag and sashayed out the door.

The city was jumping, and she had the entire night to experience it with her girls.

They met at their favorite bar, the sound of laughter and music spilling out into the street.

For the first time in a long time, she allowed herself to breathe, to let go, and to enjoy the moment.

Elisa spent her night dancing and sharing memories with her Sorors.

She felt like a weight had lifted off of her.

She was so free that her thoughts had not once drifted to Sampson.

The music was such a vibe.

The wine was steadily flowing.

The laughter was contagious.

Her girls didn't bring up the guys at all.

She was grateful for the unspoken grace they were giving her.

The night had ended and she absorbed the moment.

Her face had a permanent smile from the laughing she had done.

Spending time with her girls was much needed and she was honestly looking forward to many more nights just like this.

The ladies decided to plan another outing in 30 days.

They finally made it out of the group chat and were now sealing the deal for the next meet up.

The ladies decided to ride share so no one would be dropped off alone.

The lingering laughter filled the car on the ride home.

They shared stories of how they went through the pledging process.

They were all grateful for their sisterhood.

Elisa was in the heart of the city center in Philly.

It was booming.

Therefore, she was the first drop off.

As soon as she exited the car, she felt her stomach speaking to her.

She decided to walk the next block to her favorite food truck.

It was calling her name, and she was more than ready to indulge.

As she reached the food truck the memories of her and Sampson stopping there after nights on the town or long runs came back.

She couldn't help but smile at those memories.

This was our spot; she laughed to herself.

The nostalgia she could not ignore as she ordered and stepped aside to wait for her order.

It was a busy night.

She took in the people laughing, music playing from nearby buildings, and the horns of cars passing by.

Then there was a sound that made her freeze right where she was.

A voice that could not be mistaken.

The cadence of his words.

The tone.

Without a doubt she knew that it was Sampson.

She could not, nor did she want to turn around.

She finally got the courage to confirm what she already knew.

As she lifted her head their eyes instantly met.

There he was standing only a couple steps away.

His face went from actively engaged in conversation to completely focused on her.

Elisa could not move.

Everything around her was a blur.

In that moment she did not hear or see anything else but Sampson.

CHAPTER 3

The Run- In

As Elisa stood there frozen for what felt like 20 minutes, she finally gathered herself only to realize that there was a woman standing beside Sampson.

The life had been sucked out of her in that moment.

She felt like she had just been hit by a Mack truck going full speed.

After not seeing him for nine months and two days, he was standing there commanding attention without trying, as usual. More handsome than she remembered and with a beautiful woman by his side.

"Elisa," he said.

She took a deep breath, and it felt like there was a ball in her throat fighting with her for air to breathe.

Immediately her heart felt shattered.

Her stomach knotted.

And she couldn't mutter a simple reply.

How could this be happening, she cried internally.

God, do You really hate me this much, she asked silently.

But to her it was explosive.

Still standing there, mind racing, unable to form a word or even move, the universe had stopped, leaving her to feel all of the pain.

She had never thought about running into him.

And it was obvious she was not prepared to do so.

Especially under these circumstances.

"Elisa," Sampson repeated, his voice always commanding, but today there was a hint of surprise as he stepped toward her.

His voice still spoke to her.

It sent chills through her from head to toe.

The feelings she tried to forget had surfaced again.

And here she was unable to say one word, paralyzed from shock.

She blinked, trying to avoid the eruptions of emotions that she felt surfacing.

Her throat was getting tighter.

She couldn't breathe.

Her chest felt heavy.

Her heart was racing.

The weight of missing Sampson, the guilt of letting him go, everything was crashing down on her in that moment.

She wanted to scream.

Yet she could not.

She wanted to know who the woman was with him.

Still no words would come.

Finally able to take a breath, she closed her eyes as the scent of his cologne caught her attention.

How she longed to be wrapped up in his scent.

She just stared at him.

"Elisa, are you good?" he asked as he stepped forward to touch her.

She could see the genuine concern on his face.

As he asked again, "Elisa, are you good?" he grabbed her hand.

That touch sent what felt like an electric shock through her body.

The sensation was unexplainable.

He was so calm and composed.

Did he not feel the same pain she did?

She wanted to snap out of the moment as shock was turning to anger.

"Ms. Newton, your food is ready."

That was her out.

She snatched her hand from Sampson, grabbed her food from the counter, and did not turn back.

Heels pounding the pavement as she started walking as calmly but as fast as she could.

Now out of sight, she ran as fast as she could.

She ran from the pain of wanting him.

She ran from the hurt of seeing him with someone else.

She ran from her soulmate.

She ran from a life she wanted so desperately with Sampson.

She continued to run, not looking back one time.

Each step was another attempt to escape the pain that was going to erupt at any moment.

The tears began to come down like a waterfall.

She sprinted in her heels and dress while holding a foot-long cheesesteak.

She could not slow down.

She wanted to get home.

She wanted to bury herself in silence.

She didn't want a soul to see her in this state.

She finally reached the elevator.

Her legs were wobbly, barely able to stand.

As the door opened, she slid to the floor of the elevator and began crying uncontrollably.

The dam had broken.

"God, why are You putting this on me?" she cried out, her voice barely able to form as much as a whisper.

God, I was having a great time with my girls.

Of all the nights, why did You pick tonight for me to see him?

For me to sit in this pain?

She looked up to the heavens as if she was waiting for God to reply.

But there was nothing but a deafening silence that continued to take her breath away.

She crawled up in a ball, knees to her chest, trying to shrink herself so the pain would diminish.

As the elevator door opened, she nearly crawled to her door.

Unsteady.

Her head overflowing with thoughts.

Nothing was making sense.

As she opened the door all she could do was think of Sampson.

Noticing the woman that stood beside him, she began to feel anger along with the pain.

She closed the door behind her and fell right at the doorway.

She didn't feel how cold or hard the floor was.

She lay there and began to cry out in agony.

The pain in her chest was nothing but a painful and broken heart.

Her pain filled the open space in cries that echoed throughout the loft.

She grabbed her heart almost like she was trying to prevent it from shattering into pieces.

"God, what did I do to deserve this?"

Still crying.

Still in pain.

And still no reply.

God had forgotten about her, she thought.

And she cried right there on the floor.

"Why didn't you save me... save me, Sampson?"

The final words she could manage for the night.

The burnout from crying had overcome her.

She was now crying silent tears, just praying sleep would consume her and take the pain away as quickly as possible.

With her luck she had no faith that it would happen.

Not tonight.

Not tomorrow.

Deep down she knew that until she faced what she was running away from, the pain would always surface.

As she stretched her body was sore everywhere.

As she opened her eyes, she realized she was still on the floor, never making it past the entry.

Her small clutch had been her pillow.

The leather stained from her tears.

The stains reminded her that yesterday was not a figment of her imagination.

It was very real.

Sampson had moved on.

But her love had not.

She had run into Sampson.

And he had moved on.

The acknowledgment that he had moved on stung her heart like a million bees.

And she was deathly allergic to bees.

She remembered the woman being beautiful, but her face would not come to her.

Elisa was grateful for that so her face wouldn't haunt her.

Sampson's face was working overtime.

She couldn't add any more torture.

Elisa, get up, she said to herself in disgust.

She decided to do what she always did to clear her mind.

Run.

Sore.

Stiff.

Eyes swollen.

Yes, a run would help.

She changed her clothes, laced up her running shoes, and headed out the door.

As she began to run every step was another attempt to outrun the pain.

Outrun the hurt.

Yet this run felt different.

It felt like the pain was growing.

She pushed through the pain of her body, the pain of her heart, and just kept running despite it all.

As she ran, she could feel the moment he touched her hand to make sure she was okay.

She could hear his voice.

The way his lips formed each syllable of her name.

For a moment Elisa held her chest right at her heart, her attempt to physically trap the pain and the memories.

Now the steps started to feel like longing, so she decided to pick up the pace.

Her thoughts shifted to not stopping her pace.

This gave her a moment to breathe.

She wished she could forget it all.

Her body was at the point of exhaustion.

She stopped, put her hands over her head to catch her breath, and just stood there.

Stuck in a gaze.

But not really looking at anyone or anything.

Chapter 4

The Aftermath

Sampson

He sat there, the night replaying over and over in his mind. It was like binge watching a series you couldn't turn off.

Days later, he was exhausted from being up all night. Seeing Elisa had stirred everything he felt for her. The reality was that his feelings had never gone away, a force deep and unexplainable.

She was beautiful, stunning even though she couldn't manage to say a word. His heart had never truly let her go.

Instantly, he wanted to run after her, but he paused.

He wanted to respect her and what she was going through.

Still, seeing her in distress, he turned to his date, Kylie, and told her he would be right back.

He followed Elisa from a distance.

She was anxious, moving faster than he expected.

He laughed briefly at how quickly she moved, and how hard it was for him to keep up.

She hurried into her building. He measured his steps carefully. He didn't want her to see him, but he needed to make sure she made it home safely.

By the time he reached her door, she had already gone inside.

All he could hear were her yells and cries.

Her words weren't clear, but her agony was.

Then her voice broke through, raw and desperate.

"Why didn't you save me, Sampson?"

The pain in her voice struck him to his core. He leaned against her door, closing his eyes, taking in all that she was feeling.

He sat there as her anguish overtook him.

He felt helpless.

Tears streamed down his face as he leaned back against her door. He wanted to break it down, to pull her into his arms, to comfort her.

But a voice stopped him.

"Son, not now."

He remained leaning on the door, his heart breaking alongside hers.

Then his phone rang.

It pulled him from his thoughts.

He stood, pressed his head against the door one last time, wiped his face, and made his way back to Kylie, leaving a piece of his heart behind.

On the way back, he sighed deeply. He knew it would be the end for him and Kylie.

His feelings for Elisa were undeniable. He would never intentionally lead someone on.

His heart wasn't ready to love anyone else, and he accepted that.

Turning the corner, he saw Kylie still standing by the food truck.

She looked furious, and rightly so.

Her face said everything her words did not.

"Take me home," Kylie demanded.

They rode in silence.

When they arrived, Sampson tried to apologize, but Kylie cut him off, not even glancing his way.

Other than his later text apologizing, which would be their last exchange.

Elisa

Elisa struggled to make it through her day. She tried to stay busy, but thoughts of Sampson were constant.

Several times she clutched her chest, as if she could feel it breaking.

How could he have moved on?

Did he stop loving her?

She had come to accept that it was finally over.

As she paced her floor, she caught her reflection in the mirror. She paused, studying the woman staring back.

Everyone always thought she had superpowers.

Always-so put together.

Independent.

Confident.

But the reflection showed someone weak, fragile, and broken.

"How do I fix this?" she whispered, succumbing to tears.

It had been two weeks since her run-in with Sampson.

Aside from work, she kept to herself.

No calls.

No texts.

No social media.

Just her sweatshirt, her pillows, and her tears.

She glanced at her phone, ringer off, and saw one hundred and eleven unread messages.

The first was from her best friend, Mia.

"Elisa, if I don't hear from you by noon, I'm doing a wellness check, and the police will be at your door."

Mia lived in Florida. Otherwise, she would have done her own wellness check.

Elisa decided to reply.

She didn't want to see anyone, especially the police.

"Hey, Me," she wrote, her nickname for Mia.

"I'm fine. I just need time to myself. You know me. I have to process things my way, usually alone.

I promise I'm okay."

"I hear you, Lye," Mia replied, her nickname for Elisa.

"You have people who love you. Don't forget that.

I'll respect your wishes for now."

Deep down, Elisa wasn't okay.

How she grew up taught her that the less people know, the less they have to talk about.

That had been her unspoken motto since childhood.

It kept people from knowing the truth, but not from talking.

When people don't know, they make up things.

She needed to run.

And she did.

She found herself on the same park paths she and Sampson used to run.

It wasn't her original plan, but the familiar trail called to her.

A place where she had always felt safe.

She could almost feel Sampson's presence, as if he were waiting, unchanged.

But everything had changed.

He was not waiting for her.

It felt unfair.

But such is life.

As she walked, she saw a couple laughing on a bench.

The sight made her heart ache.

She had once believed that kind of happiness was hers to have.

Now she wasn't so sure.

Her pace slowed to a medium walk, thoughts racing.

She had no clue what to do next or how to begin healing.

Sampson had moved on.

And she needed to find a way to do the same.

Chapter 5

Feeling Better

The same old story!

Another sleepless night with dreams of Sampson.

Though this morning, she woke up feeling protected.

In this dream, they were sitting on the beach, listening to the waves and watching the sun set.

Elisa's head rested on Sampson's chest.

He always made her feel safe and secure, and that didn't change, even in her dreams.

Today, she did not wake with tears.

She did not feel the urge to lace up her running shoes and run from her pain.

Instead, she reached for her Bible.

And turned to the book of Psalms.

She remembered her childhood pastor telling her, when she went off to college, that Psalms was her prayer book and would get her through any situation.

She hadn't taken that advice then, but now it felt like the perfect time. Life's challenges had given her more reason to strengthen her faith.

She made it a habit not just to read the Word but to reflect, ask questions, and search for deeper meaning.

"The Lord is my shepherd…" she read aloud, her voice steady but questioning.

 "What does that even mean? Does it mean He's guiding me?"

This process allowed her to meditate, gave her clarity in some situations, and highlighted areas she needed to revisit.

Some days, reading the Word stirred a mix of emotions, sadness, anger, and happiness.

Her tears of sorrow were fewer now.

Though her heart still ached for Sampson, she could not let him go.

It had been nearly four months since her run-in with Sampson at the food truck with his new girlfriend.

She still thought of him almost daily, but today she wondered if he was happy.

He was such a good man; he deserved happiness, she thought. But the idea of him finding that happiness with someone else sent a sharp stinging pain through her heart/

 She shook her head, trying to erase the thought.

Glancing in the mirror as she got ready for work, a memory of Sampson caught her off guard, and she chuckled.

It was something so childish.

One day as she was ending a phone call with Sampson, she blurted out the word "O'Toodles!" instead of goodbye, mimicking the Mickey Mouse Clubhouse.

Sampson had laughed uncontrollably, and soon they were both in literal tears.

What would be insignificant to anyone else was a forever memorable moment for them.

If she called him now and said "O'Toodles," she could guarantee he would just start laughing.

While making her bed, Elisa did something she hadn't in ages.

She knelt on the side of the bed, facing the mirror.

She prayed—not for herself, not for her pain, but for Sampson.

"God," she began, her voice shaky.

"I really do not know what to say other than I want him to be happy.

Please give him peace, give him joy. Even if it's not with me, Lord, bless him. He deserves it. Amen."

She sat in silence, hoping the phrase "He knows my heart" was true. Psalms 61 came to mind:

"Hear my cry, O God; listen to my prayer. From the end of the earth, I call to you when my heart is faint. Lead me to the rock that is higher than I."

The words hit her hard. Repeating them, her tears flowed freely, no longer tears of pain, but of release.

She spoke to God simply, like He was a friend and confidant. Warmth filled her body. She had never felt this connected to herself and to God before.

Arriving at work, she felt light, free, and glowing. Her assistant, Jennifer, noticed immediately.

"Good morning, Ms. Newton," Jennifer said, smiling. "You are glowing, girl."

Elisa laughed. "What's on my calendar today?"

Jennifer hesitated. "Well… you have a morning meeting with CS Enterprise at 9 a.m., 10:30 with Mr. Franklin, and a lunch invite from an old friend."

"And who is this old friend?"

Jennifer closed her eyes briefly, bracing herself before saying "Sampson."

Elisa stood in surprise. Calmly, she said, "That's cool. I'll let you know what I decide."

She walked into her office, still in high spirits, and shut the door.

A brief smile crossed her face, then a frown. Anger rose.

"Why didn't you save me?" she whispered.

She paced, questioning why he hadn't fought for her, why he hadn't known she was lying when she said she didn't love him.

Sampson was too good to be true. She had always felt unworthy of him, believing he deserved more than her scars and brokenness.

Her outer composure belied the chaos inside.

Elisa buried herself in work, but her thoughts ran wild. Fear and doubt filled her office. She knew she had to confront her walls and her wounds, though anger was easier to hold than the truth.

A knock on her office door and Jennifer's voice came from the other side, asking if she could come in.

"Ms. Newton, would you like me to confirm your lunch plans for today? "

Elisa did not even pause before responding. "Would you tell Sampson that I respectfully decline the offer for lunch today?"

Jennifer hesitated. "Should I give him a reason?"

Elisa simply replied, "No" and continued to bury herself in her work.

Exiting work, she sat in her car, consumed by her swirling emotions. She muttered to herself:

"Why didn't you just go to lunch with him?

Weren't you just crying your heart out for this man?

Why are you throwing up this wall again?

Elisa, you are your own worst enemy."

She turned the music up and sang at the top of her lungs to drown out her thoughts. The anger softened, now replaced by regret.

Perhaps a missed opportunity to reconnect with the man she loved.

The heaviness of that thought followed her up all night.

At her loft, she sat staring blankly, torn between pride, brokenness, and longing.

She knew she would eventually have to face her truth, but for now, she allowed herself to feel the pain of her own actions.

Chapter 6

The Refusal

Sampson

Sampson sat on his front porch listening to the trees whistling from the wind.

Staring at the leaves yet his thoughts of her refusal to have lunch with him were heavy on his mind.

Did she really hate me that much, is her heart really this cold? …....He knew better.

Elisa was the sweetest soul.

What is really going on with her is the question that filled his mind relentlessly.

He was trying to make his way in her presence in hopes of figuring it out.

He sat there running his finger through his beard, which was one of the things he would do when he was frustrated, or when he felt his anxiety creeping up.

Today he found himself in his feelings a bit saddened, a bit hurt and the uncertainty was taking its toll on his heart.

Sampson was not an impulsive man; he was calculated, someone that thought everything out in advance.

But today his longing for her overpowered his usual restraint. Just to be rejected.

Unsure of his next move the rejection of today had played on him more than he realized.

 In the moment he didn't know if he wanted to give up and accept that this may truly be the end of them.

Now twirling the strands of his beard in pure doubt and uncertainty.

In a moment of clarity something tugged at his heart.

It was quiet yet persistent voice that told him "Don't give up."

He lay there on his porch, taking in the breeze, drawing a deep breath as he tried to quiet his emotions so he could think clearly.

"She is worth it," he said aloud.

"She is worth it," he repeated, louder this time, the second declaration was an affirmation of what he already knew.

She was indeed worth it.

He knew she loved him as much as he loved her, but how he would get through to her, he had no clue.

Still, he would figure it out. He was going to be obedient to that voice that told him not to give up.

He was not ready to let go!

Elisa

After a long day of work Elisa felt good to be home somewhat relaxed.

She took in the beauty of nature as she sat on her couch looking out the windows.

The view was beautiful; she hadn't fully realized its true beauty before now. Today was better than yesterday but she could not escape her feelings, today she felt alone.

Today her ache for Sampson grew stronger, the pain held a relentless grip, and her heart was the target.

She wanted to scream until there was nothing left inside her.

The what ifs were gut-wrenching.

She replayed the passion they had shared, remembering how their first kiss had sent chills racing over her body.

A faint smile touched her lips as she thought about him lifting her over the fence of that downtown restaurant on their first date.

He had literally swept her off her feet.

It was the first time in her life she had ever felt protected by a man, and the way he loved her afterward only affirmed that he always would.

How could she ever let go of the passion, the safety, and the peace he gave her?

My goodness, she thought, I never will.

"Why Elisa - if you feel so strongly why did you refuse to have lunch"?

"Why did you push him away"?

In that moment she realized how scared she was.

Scared - she was not enough.

Scared - he was too good.

Scared - because he didn't deserve her scars.

Scared -because eventually he would feel her shame.

One day he would see the broken piece and realize she was not worthy of him.

Now filled with heavy emotions she stared at the sky and whispered out to God.
"Help me"

She wanted him to make sense of what was going on with her heart, and her mind.

"God" she began to speak "I have no clue what to do, I feel hopeless, I feel loss, Lord show me the way. Help me to free myself from these chains I have built around myself ".

She sat there in that moment and talked to God until she did not have any other words to say.

As she decided to confront her feelings she pulled out her old journals.

In doing so she came across a handwritten letter addressed to Sampson.

Her body became tense as she realized it was a letter she had written to Sampson months ago but could not find the courage to send it.

 As she began reading the letter she realized that her refusal not to have lunch with Sampson had nothing to do with him, it was about her, and her fears and scars she wouldn't address.

Was it too late to fix it?

With a clear heart, and a clear mind, she picks up the phone.

Her hands nervously trembling as she texts Sampson's phone, not allowing her fear to hold her back.

"I want to apologize for everything." Can we talk?" She hits send.

Unsure of his response she took a deep breath and before she could exhale Sampson's name lit up across her phone.

She was in disbelief that he responded so promptly.

Though he wasn't returning her text with a text, he was calling her.

She felt a lump in her throat, she gathered herself to answer.

Terrified of what would be on the receiving end.

She braced herself before saying "Hello."

The word came out softly, her voice mixed both fear and longing.

"Elisa," he replied.

His voice was instantly familiar - deep and confident as she remembered. The voice that calmed her. The voice that protected her.

It was a voice she missed dearly.

In true Sampson fashion he did not waste time on the small talk.

His tone was noticeably clear, steady, and very sure.

"We need to talk in person. "No texts, no phone calls just us.

"I would appreciate that" she replied, her voice a notch above a whisper.

The meet up was set they would be meeting tomorrow at a local coffee shop which would be a neutral yet comfortable place to talk.

As she hung up the phone, she stood there, her eyes started to water as she was unsure of what tomorrow would bring them, but she was more than ready to face whatever that would be.

Sampson

Lying across his bed staring at the ceiling, his fingers combing through his beard.

Sampson felt anxious about seeing Elisa tomorrow.

Yet he also felt a relief to finally have this moment with her.

He was not sure if forgiveness would come easy either way, but he knew tomorrow would be one of closure or one of breakthrough.

Either way he was ready to face it.

The one thing they both realized was that it would be a true test of their love for one another.

Before Elisa got ready for bed, she decided to get her clothes ready.

Like a kid on the first day of school.

She wanted to look good but not as if she was trying too hard.

Sampson always loved her with a simple ponytail to the back and dressed down.

She decided it would be ponytail, joggers, and an oversized tee but of course she had to add her little flair to the outfit.

She was hopeful for tomorrow!

Very much so that she drifted off to sleep.

That sleep would end up being one of the best nights of rest she had had in months.

Chapter 7

The Meet Up

Her heart was racing as she stepped out the door to her loft. Now in front of the coffee shops her nerves had skyrocketed.

In one breath she wanted to turn around and run like she had become accustomed to doing.

Yet she acknowledged this is her season of growth and her old ways had costed her the man she loved.

So, today, Elisa decided to man-up and take her punches however they came.

Sampson was always early, on time was considered late.

He could have gotten there last night, as he was just that eager to see Elisa.

He needed to read her eyes as he spoke to her, he needed to gain understanding and clarity.

He got there in enough time so that if Elisa arrived early, he would still be there waiting on her. As he sat at the table waiting, he began to pray, he was ready to face this moment.

Elisa sat out in front of the coffee shop for a bit to gather herself. She looked in the mirror to give herself a pep talk. "You can do this Elisa" we are not running we are facing things head on, no matter how hard that gets.

She closed her eyes for a quick moment and said "God be with me" as she exited the car and headed in the coffee shop.

Sampson was inside and Elisa noticed him instantly. He was his typical calm, and confident self, standing to great Elisa.

Her heart dropped as he approached, the hint of his cologne lingered as he led her to a seat by the window.

Her steps were a little hesitant, but Sampson posture was assuring.

Every detail of this man whom she had loved was even more beautiful than she remembered. His tight jawline, his chocolate brown eyes, and how he always demanded attention wherever he was - and not in a cocky or boastful way. It was a natural superpower that he possessed.

Sampson looked put together on the outside but internally he was uneasy. As he guided Elisa to her seat now taking his, He held the cross around his neck and silently said Lord guide my words.

As he took his seat across from her, Elisa's nerves were visibly uneasy, yet she forced her eyes to meet his. In that moment she felt both scared, and hopeful of what was to come next.

They both ordered coffee, both of which would go untouched.

The conversation started off light as if Sampson was trying to gauge the interaction.

Which allowed Elisa to open up, her voice with a little tremble as she spoke.

Sampson was firm but gentle in his replies, which helped Elisa articulate the words she was scared to say.

"I pushed you away because I was scared," she admitted, eyes locked on the table rather than his.

Scared that I wasn't enough for you.

Scared of the darkness in my past.

Scared that one day you'd wake up and see just how broken I really am.

 You're so strong, Sampson, so good, and I kept telling myself you deserved someone whole, not someone like me."

Sampson moved closer to her, extending his hands to hers.

His eyes were fixated on each word.

He did not interrupt.

He did not dismiss what she was saying.

Instead, he sat there listening with intent. He felt the honesty of her words; she was speaking from the heart. To know she felt that way cut deep.

But her truth is what he needed; it is what has kept him up at night.

He let her finish then he inhaled before responding.

"Elisa, I need to understand why do you feel so broken, and unworthy of a solid love?

Where is this hurt coming from?

He sincerely wanted to know, just the thought was breaking his heart for her more than himself.

Tears started to well up in her eyes as she lifted her head to meet his eyes.

"I've been hurt Sampson.
More than I want to remember.

I thought by pushing you away, you would realize that I was not all what you thought you wanted.

Sampson's jaw tightened, and he began to comb his fingers in his beard.

It felt like an hour before he responded. He wanted to protect her in every way, he wanted to hold her at that moment, and to beg her to trust him and to never shut him out again, and to let her know they were going to work it out. But as much as he wanted to, he knew he could not be selfish. He knew that Elisa needed to heal from what was hurting her.

Even as strong as he was it took every ounce in him not to put his emotions on full display. Even in her vulnerability he wanted her.

He wanted her time.

Her laughter and smile.

Her walking hand in hand with him daily.

He remembered the scripture "love is patient Sampson" and in that moment he knew he had to do what was best for her even if it was not what he longed for and wanted.

"Elisa," he said as he pulled her hand to his lips and softly kissed them.

I love you, there is no second guessing that.

Yet I must be honest I can't pretend we can fix this overnight.

I need for you to find peace within yourself. I need for you to heal those things within in you that makes you feel this way about yourself.

What do you think about a therapist?" He asked gently, feeling her out.

He paused for a bit to give her a moment. She was hesitant to reply so he spoke up.

"Honestly, it has helped me process a lot of things lately, from my dad not being around, and my trying relationship with my mom. I have found myself in counseling and church weekly."

Elisa didn't want to appear irritated. He meant well, his words were sincere, yet they also pierced Elisa's pride.

She had at one point thought she was so strong that nothing phased her, but recently she has been an emotional basket case.

She wanted to be mad, she wanted to turn it around on him, but there was a hint of conviction she felt inside of her from his words.

She realized he was correct; she needed to deal with the buried yet still open wounds that had never properly healed. It was the right time.

She gave a nod "as much as I would like to fight you on this, I do feel it is time for me to fix what is broken inside of me. "

Sampson kissed her hands again and held them tighter, he knew that they were saying goodbye, yet he was trusting God to bring them back together.

He prayed that she knew that everything he was doing was to set them up for a successful forever.

They both knew it was the right thing to do. They decided to give each other space, to heal, and work on themselves separately.

They did not discuss when they would be in contact, they were going to allow things to naturally evolve.

They both left the café that day, carrying the weight of hope and love.

Chapter 8

Healing

Elisa

Therapy had become Elisa's lifeline. Each week she would grow to trust her therapist more and more.

Sitting in the chair across from Madeline saying things aloud that she hadn't dare share with another soul.

Some days the pain of her childhood was grappling, but she managed to continue to unbury the layers of hurt, the layers of shame, those very things that caused her to love the people in her life the way she had.

The repetitive meetings were strenuous, some weeks draining, other weeks a relief, each breakthrough allowed her to slowly regain pieces of herself.

There were moments of setbacks even then she still felt a weight, lifting off of her, and shame gradually leaving, some weeks slower than others but progress, nonetheless.

Journaling had become her best friend. It allowed her to see just how far she had come, while also serving as a safe outlet.

Journaling helped Elisa's trust problems as well, the less people knew about her, the less they could hold over her head.

Therefore, pouring her innermost secrets onto each page had felt like confiding in a trusted friend, one who would never repeat a word.

The healing Elisa was experiencing had now spilled over into her career. She had become more confident, no longer trying to make others see her worth because she knew her worth, she finally started to see that she was enough.

Her execution and confidence at work had captured the attention of her executive leadership. In no time this recognition had Elisa being promoted, one of the youngest yet highest paid women in the company and the region across companies in her industry.

At just 35 years young she was making great money, traveling the world professionally. For the first time Elisa was feeling freedom she could not explain, yet there was a void she didn't understand but kept pushing.

She was learning to pray for things and situation, so she prayed that the void would eventually fade, as she kept progressing and making the right choices.

Sharing in her growth she began mentoring younger employees of the firm, empowering them to feel that they too could persevere all.

Her mentoring program turned into another avenue of healing; it allowed her to see her value and that she had something meaningful to offer.

Sampson

Sampson too had been on a journey, his journey was more of a spiritual one, which led him to be more in-tuned with accomplishing both personal and business goals.

Sunday morning worship service was just not a routine for him; it had become his steady foundation. That coupled with his counseling, prayer, and bible study he finally began healing from his internal pain. The pain of a dad who was not there, and a mother who was too young to parent him.

He was attempting to build a healthy relationship with his mom. His dad was still missing in action.

He even began speaking to others about his journey, he was invited to different events around the city. He was in high demand often times turning down opportunities because his schedule stayed busy.

In this season he had become stronger emotionally and spiritually.
Anxiety no longer took residence within him.

Sampson had turned his passion of running into a lucrative business opening a specialty sports store that focused on runners.

The store provided the correct clothing; the proper running shoes he even partnered with a company to make custom shoe inserts based on body weight and different body pressure points.

No two runners were the same and these inserts would be customized for each runner.

He had become even more disciplined, something that seemed almost impossible for a man who was known for his discipline.

The preparation for opening his business had given him more purpose and his dreams were becoming reality. He was clearly focused, and it caused so many doors to open for him.

The process demanded a lot of his time and energy, and running continued to be his outlet.

His business was taking off and his faith had grown even stronger.

He focused on God and career.
He hadn't dated since Kylie.

He was also intentional about allowing Elisa space to heal.

He didn't even think about romance or dating he had allowed his faith to lead him as he continued to grow fully into the man God had called him to be.

He had found such peace in surrendering to God. It was because he trusted that his steps were ordered, and the more he stayed connected and intentional with God, God would continue to keep him aligned with his purpose.

Neither Elisa nor Sampson knew how the others were doing, yet somehow, they were both excelling and healing in their own ways, walking similar yet separate paths.

That had both in their own time come to realize that true growth requires looking within and focusing on personal healing.

Elisa

Elisa had begun to find joy in the little things she once took for granted.

Like sitting on her balcony with a cup of coffee, listening to the leaves rustle in the trees and the birds chirping as morning settled in.

In those quiet moments, she allowed herself time to reflect.

She laughed softly as she sat on the balcony couch, amazed at how much her life had changed.

Who would have ever thought Elisa would be volunteering at local charities?

Yet she found fulfillment in pouring her heart and time into the young people she served.

She was discovering a deep, unexpected peace, and it was a peace that was not tied to expectations.

She saw pieces of herself in many of the children she spoke with, and that alone gave her the strength to advocate for them, showing them what structure, work, and healing could truly look like.

After work she headed to the gym, as she was on the stairmaster a picture of her came across the tv screen.

It caused her to unmute the tv to hear what was being said.

"Meet Elisa Newton – Philadelphia's youngest partner, she is smart, she is gorgeous, she is paid, and we hear she is single."

Where is this coming from, she laughed.
She had elevated to a level in her career that she only dreamed about. Everything was falling into place.

There was no arrogance, Elisa stood there proud, "I've beat the odds" she said as she internally hugged herself.

The next morning, she had a counseling session with Madeline she wok up with the urge to discuss Patricia Newton…… her mother.

Elisa beat Madeline to her counseling office. Before Madeline could unlock the doors Elisa began rambling off. "Elisa slow down" Madeline encouraged her. Let's reserve this until we get inside my office!

Madeline takes her seat and grabs her IPAD. "Elisa why is it important to you if your mother is proud of you or not"?

Elisa for the time this morning slowed her thoughts down to think of a truthful answer to Madeline's question.

"Well," Elisa replied. "Growing up I never felt loved by my mom, she always shamed me, and she never said anything positive to me about myself".

"I guess the little girl in me always wanted to make her proud, but the grown woman in me should not care at all'.

Madeline's expression does not change, though she leans back and asks, "When you picture that little girl trying to make her proud, what does she look like to you?"

Momentarily quiet, Elisa thought back to moments in her childhood before speaking.

"I think, the little girl in me tried to earn something that was just unavailable."

I made straight A's, I ran track, I was a cheerleader, I was in the Honors Society, I played basketball which I hated, all of this too be away from home, away from her, away from Leonard.

She paused; Madeline did not interject.

"Patricia was not affectionate. She never hugged me; I don't remember her ever telling me she loved me. I felt like a burden, I never felt seen, I always just felt in the way."

Tears are now flowing. "And even feeling the way I did, I still wanted her to comfort me, for her to say Lye it is going to be okay."

"She never did."

"She would look me dead in my eyes with a stern face, and say little girl, things like that happens in every family, like it was a normal thing and that I just had to find a way to deal with it."

"Madeline "Elisa asked do you think she just didn't know how to love me?"

"It sounds to me you are trying to make sense of something that caused you deep hurt. Whether she did not know how to love you or decided not to show you she loved you, the impact on you remains the same. You felt invisible and unprotected when you needed her the most."

For the first time in a while the floodgate of tears hit. She thought of her dad, if hadn't died when she was just nine years old none of this would have happened.

"Elisa, what are you feeling now?"

Elisa now staring blankly, twirling her fingers. "If my dad Randal Newton had lived none of this would have happened." My daddy did not play any games about his butter cup" she smiled thinking about it.

I always felt so safe with my dad, almost invincible, my dad was so strong, he was so smart, he worked hard, and Patricia and I did not want for anything.

Madeline leaned back in her chair, her voice still calm and steady.

"It sounds like your father was your safe place."
"When you talk about him, you lighten up, I can hear the little girl in you finding a place to rest in your dad."

Losing someone you love so much at such a young age is a severe loss for a child. Especially because that was the person who made you feel the secure and safe "

"And sometimes a child loses the parent who provided the safety, and the love, and the affection which can make the absence from the other parent feel even deeper."

"I want you to think about this as we come to the end of our session today, could it be that part of you is not just grieving your dads passing, but you are too grieving the security and protection that your dad provided you?

"Elisa takes a moment to gather yourself, take some deep breaths, know that all of your feeling matter. "You made great progress today."

Elisa gave Madeline a wave confirming she understood.

As Madeline left the room, Elisa sat there for a minute, then proceeded to freshen her makeup, heading out the door in boss mode like the session never happened.

Sampson

Sampson had found peace in his stillness and structure.

Every morning his runs had become his meditation and prayer time.

Each morning as he ran, his body would become tired, some days exhausted which we would be due to the emotional release that he did not realize was needed.

Each day he ran for clarity, for self-reflection, and to become an overall better version of himself.

It had been several months since he and Elisa sat in that coffee shop. He missed her dearly, yet the pain had eased enough for him to finally feel some relief.

Though he had not contacted Elisa he still felt that the unshakeable bond between them still remained.

St. Matthew's Baptist Church now Sampson's safe place, a place he was free to worship, a place that he felt the power of God moving through him.

Each week he would go to both bible study and Sunday worship with a heart that was open to receive and experience God. He was grateful for his newfound self.

His business had become a hit, the focus on the customized insoles, was what took him to the next level. He went from opening his first store to having a chain business, "Run It Up" had now expanded across 4 different states.

Though there had been a lot of sweat and tears around his business it felt like the shift happened overnight.

His discipline allowed him to focus and support the quick expansion of his business. He had an effective team around him that kept the wheels turning and aligned.

His Saturday night ended with him hiring two new managers, then heading to the health food store, then home to relax for the night and prepare for church the following morning.

Sampson showered and laid across his bed and turned on the tv. He saw something that made him sit straight up. It was a picture of Elisa, and the host followed the picture with "Meet Elisa Newton – Philadelphia's youngest partner, she is smart, she is gorgeous, she is paid, and we hear she is single."

Sampson now combing his fingers through his beard. He could not help but smile at her beauty, he was proud of her in that moment. "Partner" I know that is right baby girl." He said to the tv as if she could hear him.

He was genuinely happy for her, but he couldn't help but feel a tinge of jealousy with the whole "we hear she is single" statement. Happy she was still single but jealous that this may be an invitation for other men.

Let me go to sleep, he said as he turned off the
television and lights. Sleep did not find him easily; he
spent the remainder of his night thinking about her.

Chapter 9

Meant to be Here

Elisa never really thought about attending any church, she was usually cool with watching online services most Sundays, of at all.

Regularly her assistant Jennifer would invite her to her church; she never pressured Elisa but made it her business to extend the offer.

Jennifer was the perfect assistant, she was polished, very thorough, and very serious about her faith.

Elisa loved that about her. She wouldn't beat you over the head with her bible, but if opportunity presented itself, she was telling you how good her God was.

Unbeknownst to Elisa, Jennifer had spotted Sampson attending her church on Sunday's and even attending bible study and Sunday school.

She wanted to tell Elisa, but Jennifer saw the growth in Elisa and believed in divine timing, when it was time God would align the two of them.

Elisa

It was a late Saturday night, and Elisa had laid in her bed just reflecting, she had an impromptu thought to finally take Jennifer up on her offer.

 It was late but she took a chance and sent Jennifer a text "Hey Jennifer if you are up text me the name address and time of service and I will meet you there tomorrow."

Elisa had decided if Jennifer texted her back before she went to sleep for the night that was her sign to go.

It was not even 2 minutes later that Jennifer replied with the address and time.

The next morning, Elisa pulled up to St. Matthews Church.

It had been many years since Elisa had been in anybody's church physically, and today she as walked up to the doors a hint of nervousness hit.

She was unsure of what to expect, but open to the experience.

The instant she walked through the church doors, Jennifer was there with the biggest smile that was truly genuine.

Elisa and Jennifer shared an unspoken bond because of their boss-employee dynamics. Even so, they were fond of each other and genuinely cared for each other. What they had was more than a work relationship, it was a strong, evenly felt sisterhood.

Not only Jennifer, but the greeters made her feel welcomed, as if she truly belonged there. That set the tone for her entire experience.

The music, the emotions, as the musicians played, and the praise team had the room full! Elisa felt something stirring within her, something she had never felt before and something she couldn't quite explain.

The choir was unmatched, but when the pastor began preaching, it felt as though every word of his sermon was meant just for her.

Tears began to fall, and instead of wiping them away, she allowed herself to fully embrace the moment.

The sermon was about restoration and how God has the ability to heal broken pieces and make a person whole again.

The pastor spoke about identity, reminding the congregation that people are not defined by what others say they are or should be, but by who God created them to be.

He preached about the love that fills emptiness the kind of love only God can give, a love that does not leave scars or make you feel empty.

Tears began to fall. Elisa, who was never comfortable with others seeing her vulnerable, found that at this moment she simply did not care.

The words spoke directly to her heart. Shock waves moved through her body. She had heard of the Holy Spirit before and wasn't sure she fully believed, but as she stood there, belief covered her, and she allowed herself to release everything she had been holding in.

She felt the power of God moving through her.

When the pastor called those who wished to come to the altar, Elisa felt her feet move before she could even think.

In an instant, she found herself at the altar, surrounded by others seeking something from God. Some stood with their heads bowed, others cried out, while some lifted their hands high, but all were there with hearts ready to receive.

The authority and power behind the pastor's prayer moved Elisa in a way she had never experienced before.

"Lord, touch every soul here today," he began, calling on God. "Heal childhood wounds. Break every chain of fear, shame, and unworthiness. Let Your people know they are enough because You are enough. Restore, redeem, and renew right now, in the mighty name of Jesus."

By this point, Elisa was silently sobbing. The prayer reached deep into her spirit. Then the pastor said, "Now I need you to grab the hand of the person standing next to you and repeat after me…"

Elisa instinctively reached to her right without opening her eyes. As she reached to her left, her hands began to shake, and the hand that clasped hers gave an affirming, yet comforting squeeze.

Still in the moment as the pastor is praying over those at the altar. The same hand gave a comfortable squeeze this time causing her to turn her head.

When she looked to her left, her legs nearly buckled. The eyes staring back at her were the same eyes that visited her dreams night after night. It was Sampson.

Both met with shock for a moment, everything around them was obsolete. Their gaze was filled with a new feeling, it was bold, but it was undeniably unshakable.

Regaining their focus back to the man of God, still holding hands. In unison they repeated after the pastor. "Lord, I surrender, Lord I believe, And Lord in you I am healed, I am renewed, and I am covered. "

There was no doubt Elisa was supposed to be there. It was not forced, no other words than - divine timing.

Everything that happened in that moment had been because it was meant to happen. They say God, and His timing was perfect, no one but him could have orchestrated this scenario.

As they released hands, their eyes met, they gave each other an affirming nod as they headed to their seats. Jennifer eyes pouring like a water fountain as she her sister girl made it back to her seat. Jennifer felt the beauty of the moment, she knew Elisa's heart needed it.

Everything after altar call had been a blur, however she knew that moment was only something that God could have arranged.

As the benediction ended Elisa gave Jennifer a hug that was so tight, she didn't speak a word, but Jennifer knew that hug was an intimate thank you.

The ladies both headed out the sanctuary.

Sampson moving with intention, navigating through the crowd until he spotted Elisa.

"Elisa" Sampson said, his voice commanding the room as it was filled with strength and emotion.

Elisa did not say a word; she just instinctively walked right into Sampsons arms. And as she did, she felt that little girl inside her being protected, she was safe.

He lifted her off her feet, in that moment they felt connected, no words spoken they just took in the moment.

Those few minutes of embrace released, uncertainty, and longing.

As they finally released from each other's embrace, their tear-filled smiles had people around them smiling at the wholesomeness.

Finally, Sampson spoke "Let's talk" Elisa confirmed with a nod; her heart was too full to even form a sentence.

"Brunch?" he suggested, another nod in agreement from Elisa as Sampson walked her to her car.

Chapter 10

Healing Together

The day felt like God was smiling down on them, Sampson, and Elisa set outside on the quaint restaurant it had the perfect aesthetic for intimate brunch date.

The sunlight hit the patio perfectly, not too much to overwhelm you but just enough to have your skin glistening.

The tables were beautifully set with crisp white linens, gold polished silverware, tasteful floral center pieces and elegant scents that set the tone for the meal.

As they set there, remembering olds times, there was an ease in the air, no anxiety, no heaviness, no looming sense of what was coming next. It felt good and it felt right.

Sampson rubbing Elisa hands glowed as he took in her beauty.

"Elisa," Sampson said she could see the sincerity in his eyes.

"Let's start over, and let's do it the right way" With honestly, trust, patience, love. And God being the center."

As her eyes begin to well up with tears it was not because of sadness or uncertainty, but it was for peace and confidence in them as a unit.

"Sampson" I would love that.

As they sat across from one another they were holding hands and smiling, not chasing out of need, but moving forward in what was meant.

No longer chasing love, this time they were building it!

Leaving brunch Elisa couldn't keep her joy to herself. She could scream to the heavens how happy she felt.

So many years of convincing herself she was not worthy of a healthy love, because of how her pass had tainted her. God's grace had definitely revealed itself to her, she was ecstatic she now had a second chance at love, and with her soulmate.

She decided to text her girls "Ladies, "Short notice, but I have some amazing news meeting at Tranquil Spa in 2 hours if you can.

The replies trickled in; they didn't question; they just showed up happy and ready to support their friend for whatever reason she would be sharing with them.

After months of dealing with her brittle heart they were ready to absorb anything that brought her a lick of happiness.

As they were all there waiting, anxious to hear the news, but patient not to ask due to her fragility lately.

 Elisa was waiting for someone to ask but couldn't hold it any longer.

She rambled the words "Sampson and I are back together, this time starting over but it is a little different he gets the healed Elisa, and then she elaborates on how it was God who brought them back together at St Matthew's.

Each of the ladies was happy for her, they knew their girl needed to work on what was troubling her first! But they always felt that her and Sampson were meant to be together, and it was just a matter of time.

Elisa was genuinely happy from the inside out. She was surrounded by the love of her friends there was a glow about her that you couldn't help but notice.

"Ladies "she said. "Thank you for showing up I know I have been difficult to deal with lately. But I want to assure you all that this love is not just about Sampson and I getting back together. What it is, is a testament of healing, standing on faith and a true example of the statement that God's timing is perfect."

Ever since that day Elisa and Sampson were inseparable, they were committed to one another, helping each other grow in their respective careers, grow with each other, and with their walk in God.

Not only were their careers booming, so was their love for one another. Elisa went from not going to church at all to going to church two times a week.

They had come the most popular couple at St. Matthew's they were even serving alongside of one another.

They weren't engaged but knew that was next steps for them, therefore they started attending Christian couples therapy in addition to their own personal sessions.

They learned to forgive completely, they learned to trust one another, but most importantly something that was new for both of them is they learned how to keep God in their center of their relationship.

They felt stronger together, confident in their healing and growth. What once felt so broken was now stronger than ever.

This couple had now become #coupleGoals, a testament of healing and renewal. They were a witness of how God can restore. They were affectionately called the "Destined Duo" by Jennifer because she could see they were destined for greatness, not just in their relationship but in every aspect of their lives.

That name begins to stick beyond the walls of St. Matthew, everywhere they began going, people were saying that's, that couple the "Destined Duo" social media played a big part in that.

Due to the rise in their social media presence the couple's notoriety grew. News outlets and local radio stations were lining up to interview them.

Their story had become more than a success story but also a testament of how they found purpose in healing. One headline read Purpose, Partnership, and Prosperity- The "Destined Duo" who found purpose in the journey.

The couple remained grounded, they prayed together, they grew together, they shared their love in their community, in mentoring, and even in their business. They didn't allow the noise to cause them any distractions.

Early one Saturday morning they would have their first of many live interviews together.

They both sat side by side in the studio, both confident but nervous, which they hid very well.

The Segment was titled "**A Love Restore the Power of Faith and Redemption**".

Tami: Elisa, Sampson, thank you so much for being our guest here today. Your story is the big talk of the city.

Not only have you inspired many, but you also give others hope. With your story of success in careers, and restoration in love, "tell us what changed, and made this time different"?

Elisa was always reluctant to show her vulnerability, rubbed her hands on her lap and found the nerve to speak up.

 "Truthfully, we stopped trying to build something without a foundation. We had to find healing within ourselves before we could fully love each other. I needed to face my fears, I had to understand I felt unworthy of healthy love, and why I never felt like I was enough. Therapy definitely helped me, but prayer and meditation healed me, and the time apart gave me the clarity I needed.

Sampson's eyes glistened a bit, as he realized the depths of growth in Elisa. With his confident composure he chimed in.

That is just it. Too often we try to pour ourselves into someone all the while our cup is on E. I needed the time to grow beyond being a provider, I had to surrender to God, and he showed me that leading starts with humility. And when God lead us back to one another at church I knew that was God. It was not chance, it was not luck, it was all God.

Tami: couldn't help but beam with pride. "That is a strong statement" Many people separate and never find their way back. Give advice to someone who is praying for not only reconciliation but also restoration with someone they love?"

Elisa voice cracked as she started to speak, she felt the weight of the words coming out of her mouth.

"I have to say that you have to stop chasing those things that's broke and start healing those things that are within you. What you pretend or try to convince yourself what doesn't need to be fixed within God can restore that for you. When I learned that is when I was able to heal and start a new and healthy season of life."

Sampson added, "Don't forget it is always in Gods timing. His delays do not mean we are denied, sometimes He has to separate us to strengthen us.

In that instance the room fell silent, it was silence that felt sacred, the audience, the host, and even the musicians were moved.

Tami: Well guys what a beautiful reminder of a love rooted in God can stand. We would like to thank the Destined Duo for sharing such a beautiful story.

They held hands and stood giving one another a reassuring smile, realizing how God had carried them through.

Chapter 11

It's getting Hot in here.

The night was quiet; it was that kind of quietness that could bring you both comfort as well as danger.

Sampson and Elisa sat close on her balcony looking at the stars as the music played softly in the background.

The atmosphere felt electric, as their chemistry was irrefutable. The two of them reconnecting on a strong level of emotions had built up so much tension between them.

Sampson, as disciplined as he was, had finally reached his breaking point.

As he sat there with his arms wrapped around her, she slowly glided her fingers up and down his hand. As innocent and common as that was for them today it instantly stirred something within him.

He watched her quietly, taking in how she was glowing. How perfectly smooth her skin was, and how her hair flowed perfectly down her back. With that final stroke of her fingers, it was enough to take him over the edge.

He wanted her in the most intimate way.

In that moment, the atmosphere shifted, and the intensity between them deepened. Elisa felt it too. As their eyes me, time paused. Sampson's touch moved from gently outlining her face with his fingers to firmly cupping it, guiding her lips toward his.

When their lips me, the passion was undeniable, and the "want " was felt mutually. Their breathing grew heavier, and everything around them faded into the background.

Nothing else mattered: the world felt distant and irrelevant. Only the two of them existed.

Then a gut-wrenching feeling hit Elisa, speaking louder than the desire. *Not now. You made a promise, remember.*

She froze where she was, her hands still wrapped around his neck. Sampson sensed what was coming next. Their eyes fill with longing but also conviction.

"Baby…. We can't do it. Not now," she said softly, her voice still heavy with passion, yet filled with care and concern. "We said we want to do things the right way."

She knew it was the right thing to do, but even as the words departed her mouth, she had to convince herself she meant them, because every part of her still wanted him.

He pulled back, chest rising and falling. The tension in
the room was heavy, but beneath it was respect pure
and unshaken.

He nodded slowly. "You're right," he said quietly
almost embarrassed.

Elisa's eyes met him not with sadness, but with
gratitude. She loved him even more at that moment.

They sat together in silence, still close, hands
intertwined, hearts steadying again under the weight of
obedience.

It wasn't easy. It wasn't without struggle. But that night
became a turning point proof that love could be
passionate and disciplined, that desire could be real yet
submitted to something greater.

Elisa

As the soft rays of sunlight peaked through Elisa's windows, it gave her the nudge she needed to get up and start her day.

Sitting up in her bed, she shook her head, trying to clear the vivid flashbacks from the night before. She closed her eyes for a moment, re-living the electricity that sparked between them, and surprisingly she felt at peace with the decision she had made.

They had come so close to crossing that line. As much as she longed for him, she knew the wait would be worth more in the end. They were honoring God with their choice in the moment, and that is what mattered. Afterall, *Real love is patient.*

She snickered at herself, re-playing the look on Sampson's face when she reminded them of their commitment. He was not upset but it was more of a pout and that was surely a foreign behavior for him.

She had a pep in her step as she got up and got ready to meet Sampson for their run in a couple of hours.

Sampson

On the other side of town Sampson sat on the front porch of his quiet suburban neighborhood. As he read his bible and while sipping a cup of tea hot tea, he tried to remain focused. Truth be told he could not get yesterday off of his mind.

"How could I have been so weak?"

His hands over now over his face, trying to shake the thoughts. His respect for Elisa just shifted to another level for her willpower in such an intense situation.

He reclined on the patio chair, a grateful smile spread across his face as he looked up at the sky.

"She's the one," he smirked "Not just because I love her, but because she brings me closer to You. Thank You…. I just want to thank You."

A man of discipline and self-reflection - He closed his eyes and recited a quick prayer.

"Father God, give me the strength to be the leader you've called me to be. Help me continue to love her in a way that honors You. Thank You for catching us when we fall short."

With quiet excitement, he rushed back into the house to get ready. He was eager to meet his lady for their morning run.

Once dressed, he called Elisa. She answered the phone
with excitement.

"Good morning handsome."
"Good morning beautiful," he replied calmly. "I was
calling to let you know I'm on my way.
"Great because I can't wait to see you."

The was a pause before his next words. "Hey Elisa… I
just want to say thank you for keeping us on track."

Taking a deep breath before her response. "It took
everything in me, it truly wasn't easy, but I had to
follow my gut feeling.

Peace filled him, he knew that they were going to make
it.

During their mid-morning run, the air was cool, and the
birds were chirping, the rhythm of their footsteps
stamped along the path. Elisa jogged beside him
laughing softly as they teased each other about who was
setting the pace. Moment like these had become their
routine – simple, peaceful and full of unspoken
chemistry.

As Sampson studied her as she ran ahead for a moment,
he felt something settle in his heart. At that very
moment he knew he wanted to spend the rest of his life
with Elisa. His cup runeth over with certainty. Every
trial they faced, every teat they had cried. And every

season they had endured had led him to this moment of clarity.

From that day forward, he moved full speed ahead with planning his proposal. He wanted something intimate but meaningful, therefore he reached out to her Sorors for help, he wanted every detail to be just right. He wanted Elisa to be sure of his certainty as he popped the question.

On the day of proposal, he was early dressed in a crisp white shirt and a pair of khakis, fresh haircut and his beard trimmed. His nerves had met him there, so he paused to say a quiet prayer which brought him peace and calmness.

Elisa loved flowers so he chose the botanical garden. It was beautiful on its own, so he did not have to do much. As he waited patiently in the outdoor garden, the view was extremely peaceful. The colors radiated from every angle, and the soft buzz of the honeybee's filled the air hum. In the center was a clear bubble seating area, that he had set up with pink and gold blanket and accents.

As he stood there, he held a bouquet of lilies he had brought, they were Elisa's favorite flowers. She once told him they reminded her of new beginnings, and new beginnings were the season they were journeying into.

Elisa walked up and froze. For a moment, she was
completely mesmerized by how beautiful everything
was. She covered her mouth when she saw Sampson
standing there, with a sign lit up behind him that read,
Will You Marry Me? Tears instantly fell. The setup
looked like something one could only dream about,
elegant, peaceful, and you could fill that love was there.

As she made her way toward Sampson, the walk
seemed like it took an hour. When she finally reached
him, he took both of her hands. His voice was firm,
steady, yet full of emotion.

Elisa, we loved each other in our brokenness, and in our
healing. That's the kind of love that gives you strength.
You've shown me real love, a patient kind of love. And
I would do it all over again if it meant I'd get to do it
with you. The truth is, I could not imagine doing life
with anyone but you.

He got down on one knee, locked eyes with her, and
said the words with complete confidence.

"Will you marry me?"

In that moment, Elisa felt every emotion as she realized
all the moments that had led to this one. He was
definitely the man for her, and she had known that long

before she was ready to admit it. She could hardly
contain her emotions. Usually calm and collected, Elisa
was overwhelmed with joy. She jumped up and down
as tears streamed down her face.

"Yes! A thousand times yes! I will marry you!"

He slipped the ring onto her finger as a crowd of friends
and family, who had been hidden- burst into applause.
It was a moment that will live in both of their hearts
forever.

Elisa had barely noticed her ring at first. She was so in
awe of the moment and the thought that she would
spend the rest of her life with her soulmate. But once
things calmed down a little, she finally took a look. The
ring was beautiful, a pear-shaped solitaire. It was
stunning to say the least.

The night under the stars, Sampson held her close
grateful not for love alone, but grateful for God's timing
and for where they were in life that day.

Chapter 12

The Whirlwind

The engagement spread rapidly. Within hours of Sampson's proposal, photos and videos began circulating across social media. Elisa's tearful "yes," the stunning botanical garden setup, and that unforgettable moment when Sampson slipped the ring on her finger under such beautiful lighting.

The couple affectionately known as the "Destine Duo" are getting hitched #PowerCoupleGoals," one headline read. "Faith, Love, and Building Fortune: The Story of Sampson and Elisa," said another.

Their love story was no longer just their own; it had become a testimony of redemption, faith, and waiting on God's timing that would be shared by many.

Invitations for interviews begin pouring in left and right. Magazines, talk shows and podcasters were bidding for their first interview since the engagement. But the couple remained grounded, they accepted the recognition but stayed humble, and giving God credit for the blessings that continued to pour in.

They only went with a few platforms that they vetted, those who allowed them to share not just their success, but the message behind it.

"A lot of people miss the mark on love because they go into relationships unhealed. Most importantly, God isn't in the equation at all" Sampson said during an interview. "Elisa and I experienced this our first time dating."

Elisa, sitting beside him with a proud smile, added, "Our story is far from perfect, but it's purposeful. We want people to know that the real work happens before the happily ever after."

The raw honesty and transparency of this couple drew more and more people in each day. It was the story of a women who was once willing to walk away from true love rather face the scars within. But along her journey, she discovered healing, God, and favor. Now, two souls finding their way back to each other had become an inspirational love story that left people wanting to know more.

Now major media outlets have begun competing for exclusives on their wedding day. After much prayer and discussion, Sampson and Elisa signed an exclusive deal to share their wedding journey through Excellence Network on their "Love Stories" series. They also would allow a small media section for the wedding as well.

They continued making headlines in love and their careers. Elisa made history for her firm become the youngest partner, bringing the single highest revenue in

365 days ever recorded for the company. This achievement made headlines across the business world.

Her leadership and grace had earned her national recognition, still she remained humble, and very grateful.

Sampson, too, was thriving. Run It Up had exploded in popularity, now spanning across multiple cities.

Runners from all over came not just for the products, but for the experience; the way Sampson personally greeted customers, remembered names, and offered encouragement.

He'd built more than a business; he'd built a community.

Local media began dubbing him "The Gentleman Entrepreneur." His confidence wasn't loud, it was calm, rooted in faith and humility.

Everywhere he went, his presence commanded attention. He carried himself with quiet strength, the kind that came from discipline, prayer, and purpose.

When he spoke at business events or church conferences, people listened not just because of his success, but because of his sincerity.

He had quickly become the local heartthrob, admired
not just for his looks or ambition, but for the way he
loved Elisa.

Sampson spoke of her often and without hesitation,
calling her his "answered prayer." When photographers
captured them together, whether at charity events,
ministry gatherings, or simply out for dinner, his eyes
always told the same story: she was his peace, his
purpose, and his partner.

"Man, you make this relationship thing look good," his
friends would tease. Sampson would just smile and say,
When God writes the story, you don't have to force the
ending."

Social media lit up with admiration for them both.
Videos of Sampson surprising Elisa with flowers at her
office or supporting her at speaking engagements went
viral.

He wasn't just a businessman anymore he was
becoming a symbol of faith-driven masculinity, the
kind of man who led with love, integrity, and devotion.

Even through the growing fame, Sampson stayed
grounded. He continued mentoring young men at his
church, hosting small group Bible studies, and
reminding everyone that success without surrender
meant nothing.

And through it all, his love for Elisa remained at the center. Every interview, every public moment, every whispered prayer pointed back to her, the woman who had challenged him, changed him, and chosen him.

They were unstoppable, not because life was perfect, but because they walked in perfect alignment with each other and with God.

As the wedding drew closer, the passion between Sampson and Elisa grew stronger than ever. Every glance, every touch, every moment together seemed to carry a new kind of electricity.

Their love had matured, but their attraction had that deep, undeniable pull that had only intensified.

They'd waited for this, built their relationship on prayer and patience, but now the waiting had become a test of its own.

When they were together, it was as if the air shifted. Even simple moments cooking dinner, watching a movie, or talking late into the night carried an unspoken tension neither could ignore.

Sampson often found himself silently praying for strength. He loved her more than words could express, and every fiber of his being wanted to show that love fully.

But deep down, he knew what they'd promised each other and what they'd promised God.

Elisa felt it too. There were nights she'd lie awake, her heart racing just from the thought of him.

The chemistry between them was overwhelming, but so was the conviction. They had come too far, healed too much, and built too strong of a foundation to let passion lead them off course.

One evening, after another night that tested their boundaries, Elisa sat quietly on the couch, her head resting on Sampson's shoulder. The silence between them said everything.

Finally, Sampson spoke, his voice low but steady.

"Elisa… I love you too much to risk what we've built. Maybe… maybe we shouldn't spend nights together anymore. Not until we're married."

She nodded, eyes glistening. It wasn't what her heart wanted to hear, but she knew it was what her spirit needed.

"You're right," she whispered. "It's harder now than ever, but that just means it's real. Let's protect it."

They both knew the decision wouldn't be easy. There would be moments of weakness, moments of longing but there would also be peace. Because they weren't just waiting for a wedding night; they were preparing for a covenant.

And with that choice, their love deepened even more not because of passion withheld, but because of purpose pursued.

Chapter 13

The Unwelcome Knock

Everything was in place. The venue secured, the cake by the best baker in the city, the flowers were ordered, the wedding invitations themselves were the talk of the town, they were all over the news and social media.

Elisa and Sampson now dubbed the "Destined Duo" just days away from saying I do!

Elisa couldn't believe the shift in her life; she was once crying and depressed every day now she was overflowing with love and light.

Then as they say, the devil reared his ugly head - as there was a knock at her door.

Sampson had already shared his plans for the rest of the evening; therefore, she was not expecting anyone.

She called out, "Who is it?" Elisa "it's me" the muffled voice replied.

There was a hint of familiarity in the voice, and as she opened the door a ton of bricks hit her.

She could not move; she was frozen in place. The face that gave her scars of shame and made her hate herself at times was staring back at her.

He had a darkness about him, an evil spirit that followed him still to this day. Leonard, someone from her past she wishes she could forget, and she never thought she would be facing him again in this lifetime.

He was aged, unkept, and looked as if life had been hard for him, even after all these years she was still terrified of him. All of the thoughts of her childhood flashed before her.

Her innocence had been stripped from her, and the one who inflicted so much hurt, and deep scars were standing at her door; and she could not find the words to say.

"Elisa" he said softly almost as if he was trying to get her to trust him. "You have made a great life for yourself, I am proud of you, and I needed to find you to apologize, I need for you to forgive me" he pleaded.

That voice that had caused her so much pain, the disgusting things he said to her that no child should ever hear replayed in her head. Her legs felt weak, in an instant the strong, healed Elisa had disappeared.

Supposedly a close family friend, Leonard subjected her to years of pain. Too young to fully understand as a child, but the lifelong scars had settled into the corners of her soul.

Her mind raced replaying the painful moments back-to-back, each hitting her before she could process the last.

She felt shame, she felt like the little girl who was unprotected, and before she could utter a reply, she slammed her door as hard as she could.

Unsure of what to do next, she put on the deadbolt, and put a chair up under her doorknob, she locked all the windows, though she was on the top floor and there was only one way he could enter she still felt exposed.

Elisa sat in the floor, stunned, lost for words as she let the tears fall.

"God why are you allowing this to happen to me? Why now? Everything is going perfectly, why this?"

She was unable to sleep, and she sat there looking at her phone as Sampson's name appeared back-to-back, yet she watched as she was unable to answer due to the shame, she thought she had overcome.

He will never see me the same if he knows this! How can I share something so vile as this with him?

Will he still want to spend the rest of his life with me… all of the thoughts that were going through Elisa's mind.

The sunlight peaked through the window, and caused Elisa to wake, as she looked down at her hand, she was holding her taser, but her ring is what caught her attention. It was gorgeous and that was putting it mildly but suddenly that ring carried a lot of weight.

There was a soft but nervous knock at the door, tears began to fall because she knew it was Sampson. She opened the door as she knew she could no longer run. She agreed no more running.

Sampson grabbed her, "honey, what is wrong" why weren't you answering my calls? and why are you crying" His gaze remained steady but worry lingered in his eyes.

"Elisa?" he said gently passing allowing her time to reply.

She took a long, deep breath, her head now pounding, and her heart racing uncontrollably. Madaline had tried to reason with her, insisting it would be in her best interest to tell Sampson about Leonard.

The truth was, Elisa never thought it would come to this. She believed that part of her life was buried, locked away in a grave she had mentally created for it.

"No more running "she said aloud, "Sampson, there is something I have kept from you, and I need to tell you now.

Sampson grabbed her hands and looked intently, and in that moment, Elisa told him everything.

The pain, the hurt, the fear, and as she was sharing with him, felt as if it was stripping away layers of guilt, and shameful pain.

Sampson did not interrupt, he just listened. As he listened, his jaw began to tighten, he began to run his finger through his beard. Anger was boiling inside of him, anxiety had reappeared.

The only words he could get out were "I thought we said there were no secrets?"

Tears still falling down her face. Elisa replied" I guess I thought you would see me differently, that you would to feel the shame that I carry because of this."

Sampson's gaze fixated on her, the space between them felt heavy, there was still love there, but a sense of uncertainty filled the air.

Elisa reached for his hand; Sampson did not raise his hands to meet hers instead he said, "Elisa I have to go".

The door closed behind her, and Elisa felt defeated. She sat in silence and whispered, "Why didn't You save me?"

In that moment, she felt God speak gently to her heart. Elisa, my daughter, I see your pain. I have been with you, even in the darkest moments. It is okay to bring your hurt and confusion to Me.

Right then, Elisa experienced a revelation that would change her life forever!

While she was waiting for Sampson to save her, all along, it had been God that she needed.

He had been there the entire time, patiently waiting for her to see that the healing, the strength, and the love she longed for had always been found in Him.

Sampson

Sampson's hands gripped the steering wheel so hard his knuckles turned white. He was furious, he had always maintained his composure, but he was feeling out of control. He was her protector, which meant protecting her from everything- that included the pain, heartbreak, anything that could alter her spirits that was his job; yet before now he knew nothing about Leonard so how could he protect her from him?

The vision of this man who had haunted her past, was standing at her door, and that lit a fire inside of him he was unaware of. Anger, helplessness and love surged together and could not contain it another second.

He slammed his car door, screamed into the night, hollered until his voice was raw, and finally broke down in tears.

Every wail carried his pain for Elisa, his fear for her safety, and his rage at the cruelty of her having to face this trauma.

He felt powerless and that was never a problem for him. He was upset because he prided himself on being a protector but at this moment, he felt like he had failed.

Elisa

Meanwhile, Elisa sat alone in her apartment, feeling both exposed and protected at the same time. She wasn't angry with Sampson for leaving, nor was she sad. Deep down, she knew their relationship had a strong foundation. They worked hard to rebuild this beautiful thing, and she felt confident they would withstand. But most importantly she trusted God at His word.

The old Elisa would have been curled up on the floor, crying until there was nothing left. The old Elisa tried to reappear but the Elisa who was anchored in God shined through. "Girl go get your man" she said to herself, and she headed out the door. She was running today but running to him not from him.

Elisa walked on his porch, rang his doorbell anxiously. When he opened the door, his eyes were bloodshot red.

"Elisa…" he mumbled, his voice pained.

The man who had always appeared confident and strong now stood vulnerable before her. Moments later, his head rested against her chest as he cried. His tears carried pain, hurt, and anger. He was hurt that he was not there to protect her, fire in his heart at Leonard for invading her space, but pure frustration that he could not lay hands on him the way he wanted to.

He just sat there, his anger and frustration evident - the reason Elisa had kept this from him. Part of him struggled with it because whole heart believed he knew everything about the woman he loved. Yet at that moment, he respected her silence and accepted her need for healing.

He lifted his head; he tilted her chin and kissed her lips softly but with firm assurance.

"There is nothing," he said firmly, "that could ever stop me from spending the rest of my life with you."

Chapter 14

The Show Goes On

The music began softly.

More than four hundred guests sat beneath the oversized gazebo, which was beautifully draped, filled with white and pink roses. The sight was fit for a magazine.

Cameras were everywhere, the local news, radio station, and even the most watched reality show host Vira was present for the occasion.

This was not just a wedding.

It was a moment so many had waited to witness.

Sampson stood at the end of the aisle, adjusting his cufflinks, as his best man Scott stood beside him.

There was no nervousness at that moment for Sampson, he had never been more sure of anything.

Just last year he and Elisa had parted ways. But the beauty of how they reunited he stood there healed, restored and confident.

They had a real-life testimony people admired. They were young, successful, and rising. All while showing what redemption and love could look like with healing.

That's why there were so many cameras.

Why the attendance was over four hundred.

People were able to see it first-hand.

But something felt off to him.
Sampson felt it before he could place it.

An eerie feeling that caused his antennas to stand up.

His expression faintly changed.

His eyes cautiously scanned the room, trying not to appear as the groom searching for danger on his wedding day.

Row by row of familiar faces, their families, mentors, mentee, church members, and peers.

Suddenly….

A face he did not recognize.

Just 5 rows back.

The man sat awkwardly in his chair; you could tell he tried to clean himself up for the occasion yet still looking unkept.

He was too relaxed for a wedding of this magnitude. The man seemed uneasy and was not focused on the set up.

Sampson's chest tightened.

That trusting voice inside of him said.

"You know who that is."

Sampson's felt the furry inside of him while trying to keep a straight face.

Leonard.

A few days earlier.

The knock-on Elisa's door.

Sampson thought of how she must have felt, and he could hear her voice the next day as she recited to him that pain, she had buried from her childhood.

Leonard.

The man who had stolen her innocence.

The man who had never been invited into their lives again.

And yet here he was.

Sitting comfortably among their friends and family when he was neither.

Sampson's jaw tightened.

The officiant now speaking, was unaware that the atmosphere had shifted for Sampson.

Sampson took a deep breath.

Then he stepped off the platform.

Guests begin whispering.

At first it looked as if he might be greeting someone.

It was quickly realized that his expression was not of a greeting nature.

Sampson moved down the aisle with his usual confidence this time with a hint of arrogance. The place became quiet as everyone could sense an encounter.

Leonard sat tight.

He watched as Sampson was approaching him, with a hint of a smirk on his face.

Sampson stopped right in his space.

Now in the face of the man, who looked horrid, grimy and arrogant. The presence that disturbed your peace.

Sampson's voice firm, yet dangerously calm.

"Who are you?"

Leonard smirked.

"An old friend of Elisa's."

The words hit Sampson igniting fire.

People are now focused on them.

Sampson leaned closer.

"You have one minute to get out of here," he said quietly. "

Leonard's smile became taunting.

He looked around the room.

"A lot of cameras here, don't you think"? Leonard said.

He leaned forward just enough so that only Sampson could hear his next words.

"A lot of attention is on you my brotha. You wouldn't cause a scene here now, would you?"

For half a second, Sampson hesitated.

Not out of fear.

But calculation.

Then something inside him snapped.

Leonard had made one mistake.

He thought Sampson cared about who was watching more than he cared about protecting Elisa.

Sampson grabbed the front of Leonard's collar.

Guests started to whisper.

"What—?"

Before Leonard could say another word, Sampson's had lifted him straight out of the chair like a rag doll.

The room now erupts with noise.

"Oh, my goodness"

What's happening?"

Guests were in awe as Sampson lugged the slugging man out of there.

Leonard could not pull free if he wanted to.

Sampson didn't slow his pace.

His grip tightened as he drug him toward the massive doors at the back of the venue.

The crowd parted instinctively.

"Ooooh—"

"Aahh—"

Everyone is trying to understand what is going on.

Vira grabbed her camera and followed.

This was no longer a wedding moment.

This was television.

The massive doors burst open as Sampson shoved them open with his shoulder.

Leonard stumbled as Sampson yanked him forward.

Behind them, heels were clacking,

Vira now through the doors with them.

"Who is that man?!" she shouted while trying to catch her breath from running to keep up.

Sampson ignored her.

He dragged Leonard down the steps and threw him forward onto the driveway.

Leonard staggered but did not fall.

Sampson stepped closer, his shadow falling over him.

His voice dropped to a deadly whisper.

"If you ever come near Elisa again…"

Leonard dusted himself off, his look was annoyed but not afraid.

But he did not say a word.

That smirk was now gone.

Sampson stepped in his face.

"Leave."

Leonard stared him down for a couple seconds.

Then, he turned and walked away as instructed.

Behind Sampson's, Vira's voice again.

"Sampson—who *was* that man?"

Sampson stood silently, watching Leonard disappear.

Only one thought filled his mind.

Elisa! She would never have to face that man again.

Not while he had breath in him.

He turned slowly and walked back toward the venue.

Inside, four hundred guests waited.

And at the end of the aisle—

Elisa.

Chapter 15

The Heaviness of Forgiveness

The doors closed behind Sampson as he stepped back into the venue.

Four hundred pairs of eyes stared at him.

Whispers floated through the room like smoke.

The tension was thick enough to taste.

Sampson walked slowly down the aisle again, straightening his jacket as if nothing unusual had happened. His face was calm, but his heartbeat was still pounding from the confrontation outside.

The officiant cleared his throat gently.

"Well," he said with a small smile, trying to lighten the moment. "I believe we were about to witness something beautiful."

A few nervous laughs broke the silence.

The room slowly settled.

Guests sat back down.

The string quartet resumed their music.

And then the doors at the back of the hall opened again.

Elisa appeared.

The entire room stood instantly.

She looked radiant wrapped in a gown that shimmered softly under the chandelier light, her veil flowing behind her like mist. But it wasn't just her beauty that made people stare.

It was her presence.

Elisa walked with the quiet confidence of a woman who had fought through darkness and survived it.

Her eyes found Sampson immediately.

For a moment, nothing else existed.

Not the guests.

Not the cameras.

Not the whispers about what had just happened.

Just them. Sampson felt the tension in his chest release the moment she smiled.

He returned to the altar.

Elisa walked the aisle slowly, each step carrying the weight of everything they had overcome to reach this moment.

When she reached him, Sampson gently took her hands.

The officiant looked between them.

"We gather today," he began, "not just to celebrate love… but restoration."

The ceremony was simple.

Sacred.

When it came time for their vows, they had chosen to write their own.

Sampson went first.

He looked at Elisa for a long moment before speaking.

"Two years ago," he began, his voice steady, "I believed losing you was the worst pain I would ever feel. When you walked away because you didn't feel worthy of my love, it felt like my world went silent. But in that silence, God began to work on me."

He took a deep breath before continuing "He used that loss to show me who I really was, and who I needed to become. I realized there was anger in me I didn't even know were controlling parts of my life. And before I could ever stand here and truly love you the way you deserved, I had to face those things. "

The room went silent.

"What I didn't realize then was that the space you created between us wasn't just for your healing….it was for mine too. "

"And today, standing here with you, I understand something that I didn't understand before, that loving you is both a gift and a responsibility I will never take for granted. "

"And I thank God for trusting me, once again with your heart. And I vow to protect, honor and respect you for all of the days God gives us together."

Elisa's eyes glistened.

Sampson squeezed her hands gently.

"You taught me that healing isn't weakness. It's courage. And today I promise you this… I will never stop choosing you. Not in the easy seasons. Not in the storms. Not when life gets messy."

Her voice softened.

"You are my answered prayer." And I promise to honor you for all of the days God gives us together.

Elisa, a bit choked up by his words, took a minute before reciting her vows.

"When we separated," she said quietly, "I thought love had failed us."

Her voice trembled but never broke.

"But what I learned was… love doesn't fail. Sometimes people just need time to heal before they can carry it properly."

Guests nodded softly.

"You stood beside me when I finally told the truth about the pain I carried as a child. You didn't try to fix it. You just held my hand while I healed."

She smiled through tears.

"So today I promise… I will walk beside you through every version of life we face. Because what we have isn't just love."

She paused.

"It's redemption."

The room erupted in applause.

Minutes later, they were pronounced husband and wife.

The applause was more of a standing ovation.

Sampson and Elisa stood together at the altar –eyes locked, hands locked, as if the world slowed down just for them. The officiant had to clear his throat gently to regain their attention.

"May I have the rings? He asked.

"These rings," he said, holding them up, "are circles for a reason, without beginning, and without end. And just as these circles have no end may your love be eternal.

They said their I do's and gently placed their rings on each other's fingers.

Then, as if releasing everything that had held inside, they shared a kiss that made everyone gasp.

 "I now present to you, for the very first time Mr. and Mrs. Sampson Davis."

The room really erupted – cheers echoed, the clapping and whistling, and some with tissues wiping away their tears.

Sampson kissed his bride gently, sealing the moment of everything they had fought to reclaim.

The camera crew for Excellence Network who were

there documenting the wedding were in high gear. Producers whispering into headsets. Operators repositioning their lenses. A camera glided smoothly down the aisle on a rolling track, capturing the couple from all angles.

The host, Drew, stepped quietly into frame near the front, speaking softly into the camera that hovered over his shoulder. "History just happened here," he murmured, his voice controlled but excited. "What we've just witnessed isn't just a wedding, it's a full-circle moment for two people whose journey of healing has inspired thousands."

Another camera zoomed in on Elisa's radiant smile as she laughed softly at something Sampson whispered in her ear.

Guests leaned into the aisles; phones raised despite the professional cameras documenting every second.

One producer signaled toward the balcony camera.

"Get the wide shot," she whispered urgently.

Above them, the overhead rig slowly panned across the entire venue, capturing four hundred guests standing in celebration, the sea of white flowers.

Sampson and Elisa.

Victorious.

The officiant approached them quietly.

"We'll take a brief intermission before the reception begins," he said with a smile.

Sampson nodded.

Elisa took one last glance around the room.

For a moment, she looked almost overwhelmed, not by the spectacle, but by the meaning of it.

Sampson squeezed her hand.

"You good?" he asked softly.

Elisa nodded.

"Better than good."

Nearby, the camera crew captured every second of their walk down the aisle as husband and wife.

Applause followed them all the way to the doors.

And as they stepped out of the ceremony hall together, the production team buzzed with excitement.

Because they all knew something.

They had come expecting to film a beautiful wedding.

But what they were witnessing was something much deeper.

A story of restoration.

One that millions would soon watch unfold. As Sampson and Elisa stepped through the doors at the end

of the aisle, applause still echoing behind them, the production crew moved with quiet urgency.
Camera operators repositioned themselves like a well-practiced dance, capturing every angle of the newly married couple as they paused briefly in the grand foyer.

But not everyone behind the cameras shared the same calm focus.

Vira did not believe in quiet moments.

Vira the face of the reality tv stood near one of the side columns, microphone already in hand, her sharp eyes scanning the room like a hawk that had learned to smell drama before it even landed.

She was stunning, polished, and unapologetically curious.

And she had built her entire career on knowing exactly when a story was about to explode.

A cameraman beside her adjusted his lens.

"You think that thing earlier with the guy Sampson dragged out is going to make the cut?" he whispered.

Vira gave him a sideways glance.

"Oh, sweetheart," she said smoothly, fixing a loose strand of hair. "That's not just making the cut."

She smiled slowly.

"That's the episode."

Behind her, another producer stepped closer.

"Remember, we're focusing on the love story," the producer reminded quietly. "Healing. Redemption. That's the angle."

Vira nodded politely.

But her eyes had already drifted back toward the reception hall doors where guests were beginning to move toward the cocktail hour.

"Yes," she said sweetly.

"Of course."

Then she leaned slightly toward her cameraman.

"Keep the camera warm tonight."

The cameraman frowned.

"Why?"

Vira tilted her head toward the entrance where guests were still whispering about the earlier incident.

"Because weddings like this?" she murmured.

"They never end with just one surprise."

She glanced toward the hallway Sampson and Elisa had disappeared into.

Then toward the ballroom where the reception would begin.

And then back to the entrance doors of the venue.

Her instincts were buzzing.

"Trust me," she said under her breath.

"Tonight isn't over."

She lifted her microphone, flashing her signature television-ready smile as another camera light blinked on.

Because if anything dramatic happened.

Vira would be the first one there to capture it.

After a brief intermission, the venue transformed. Where the ceremony had been soft and elegant, the reception was breathtaking.

Crystal lights shimmered across the ceiling like stars.

The scent of gourmet dishes drifted through the air.

And in the corner of the grand ballroom, a live jazz band played smooth, velvet melodies that wrapped around the laughter of the crowd.

Saxophones.

Piano.

Soft percussion.

It was the kind of reception most couples only dreamed about.

Guests danced.

Servers floated through the crowd carrying trays of incredible food.

Cameras captured every moment of joy.

But for Sampson and Elisa, the world had shrunk again.

They were sitting together at their sweetheart table, laughing quietly, occasionally stealing glances at one another like two teenagers who still couldn't believe they had made it here.

For the first time all day, Sampson felt completely relaxed. He leaned back in his chair, watching Elisa laugh with one of her bridesmaids.

Then the room shifted again.

He felt it before he saw it.

Sampsons eyes drifted toward the entrance of the reception hall.

A man stood in the doorway.

Older.

Weathered.

Nervous.

Sampson froze.

His father.

He hadn't seen him in years.

The man who had disappeared from his life when he
was barely a teenager now stood awkwardly at the edge
of the celebration, clutching his jacket like he wasn't
sure if he belonged inside.

Sampson slowly stood.

Elisa noticed immediately.

"What is it?" she asked softly.

Sampson didn't answer.

Before he could move toward the door

Another voice cut through the room.

"Elisa…"

The word was slurred.

Heads turned.

Leonard stumbled into the reception hall.

He no longer had the smug confidence he carried earlier.

His shirt was wrinkled.

His face flushed.

His eyes glassy with alcohol.

Guests gasped.

The jazz band continued playing in hopes of distracting guests.

Leonard staggered forward, nearly losing his balance.

"I just… I just need to talk," he said weakly.

Sampson's fists clenched instantly.

He stepped forward, rage rising in his chest.

"You shouldn't have come back."

Leonard raised his hands shakily.

"I know… I know… I messed up."

His voice cracked.

Sampson was already moving toward him when another voice spoke.

"Sampson."

It was his father.

Sampson turned sharply.

The older man stepped closer, his eyes heavy with regret.

"Son… I know today ain't the day for this… but I had to come."

Sampson stared at him in disbelief.

"You disappeared for twenty years," Sampson said quietly.

"And today is when you decide to show up?"

His father swallowed hard.

"I've been carrying that shame every day."

Before Sampson could respond, Leonard collapsed into a nearby chair.

"I'm dying," Leonard blurted suddenly.

The room went silent.

Sampson frowned.
Leonard wiped his face with shaking hands.

"Doctors say… not much time left."

His voice cracked again.

"I came because I can't leave this world with what I did to her."

Sampson's anger surged again.

"You should've thought about that years ago."

Leonard lowered his head. "I know."

At that moment, Elisa stepped forward.

Her voice was calm.

"Sampson."

He turned to her.

The room watched carefully.

Elisa walked slowly toward Leonard.

Every step carried a quiet strength that silenced the entire reception.

She stopped in front of him.

Leonard couldn't even look at her.

"I came to ask… forgiveness," he whispered.

Sampson started to speak again, but Elisa gently placed a hand on his arm.

Her voice was steady.

"We forgive," she said.

The room seemed to hold its breath.

Sampson looked at her, stunned.

Elisa continued.

"Not because what happened didn't matter," she said softly.

"But because forgiveness is what we need to heal."

Leonard finally looked up, tears streaming down his face.

"You forgive me?"

Elisa nodded slowly.

"Yes."

Then her voice became firmer.

"But forgiveness from me doesn't save your soul."

Leonard blinked.

Elisa looked him directly in the eyes.

"You need to repent." Her words carried weight.

"You need to ask God for forgiveness. He's the only one who can save you."

Leonard broke down completely.

A few feet away, Sampson's father wiped his own eyes quietly.

The band is still playing.

Four hundred guests watched a moment no one expected to witness.

Not drama.

Not revenge.

But something far more powerful.

Mercy.

And for the first time that night

The chaos faded.

Because healing had just walked into the room.

Elisa no longer allowed Leonard to control her. She could never forget the pain he had caused, but she realized that holding onto it almost cost her the best man she could have ever dreamed of.

Chapter 16

The Honeymoon

The moment they had longed for had finally arrived. Their wedding had ended at 10 PM.

And almost immediately, the bride and groom were whisked away to begin their honeymoon, their first night as husband and wife.

Their destination: the breathtaking shores of Aruba.

Their bags were packed, and after a quick change from wedding attire to travel wear, they were driving off in a clean all-white Rolls-Royce Phantom.

It was courtesy of the Excellence Network for the evening, and its polished surface was glistening under the night lights.

The drive to the airport felt like an eternity.

They held hands, fingers locked together as if letting go could undo every prayer that had brought them together.

Sampson rested his head lightly against Elisa's, and she leaned into his warmth, wrapped up in the quiet intimacy.

Every affectionate touch, and every quietly spoken word, made the reality of their union feel more sacred.

The flight seemed endless, but neither minded.

They were curled close together in the dim glow of the cabin lights, hearts racing in tandem.

Soft laughter and murmurs passed between them as they traced patterns on each other's hands and arms.

It was the first time in their lives they could be completely themselves, free of expectation, free of the past, fully surrendered to the night ahead.

The events that had led up to the day had them both beaming with joy and, to say the least, utterly exhausted.

Every laugh, every tear, every blessing they had received earlier that day weighed gently on their hearts. On the plane the comfort of being together wrapped around them like a soft blanket.

Curled up against each other, their bodies pressed close they surrendered to the exhaustion of the day. Neither moved, neither stirred, letting the quiet intimacy and the soft hums of the flight cradle them for the duration.

Arriving at the resort, they were greeted by a glass of wine. Neither of them were regular drinkers, but the indulgence felt fitting.

The air smelled of salt water and tropical flowers, warm and intoxicating.

They tapped their glasses softly, smiling at each other "To Mr. and Mrs. Davis" they said in unison.

Their suite was breathtaking.

Floor-to-ceiling windows opened to a terrace with a swim-up pool that glimmered in the moonlight.

An indoor and outdoor shower promised indulgence, while the ocean stretched endlessly before them.

As the door closed shut, the applause, music, and laughter of the wedding faded into the past, leaving only the quiet, sacred world they would now share.

Elisa slipped her hand into Sampson's, and he held it as if letting go might undo every step that had led them to this night.

There was no rush, only deliberate, lingering movements every glance, every touch, was infused with desire and reverence.

Every heartbeat between them was a silent prayer of gratitude, a celebration of love finally fulfilled.

Their lips met in a kiss that deepened, slow and consuming, as if trying to memorize every inch of each other.

It was tender, yet it carried the unspoken longing of months of waiting and healing.

Their movements were slow, deliberate, an unspoken rhythm that only the two of them understood.

Sampson's hands cupped her face, and Elisa's hands tangled in his hair, their bodies pressing close, fitting together as if they had always been made for this moment.

Every touch was a promise, every sigh a renewed vow in the quiet intimacy of their room.

Time ceased to exist.

The gentle crash of waves below, the scent of salt and love in the air, the warmth of the pool and candlelight, all became a backdrop to their union.

Every kiss, every embrace, every whispered name was a sacred act, a physical prayer honoring the covenant God had blessed them with.

As they finally lay together, hearts beating in perfect harmony, they understood the depth of what they had been waiting for.

This night was more than passion, it was the consummation of faith, patience, and love.

Every touch and every glance was a testament to God's timing, a celebration of two souls who had healed, waited, and chosen one another in faith.

In that quiet, moonlit suite, they discovered that love, when patient and surrendered, is powerful.

Chapter 17

The Morning After

Morning sunlight crept quietly through the tall curtains of the bridal suite.

Stretching across the polished floor and slowly climbing toward the large bed where Sampson and Elisa lay wrapped in the peaceful silence that only comes after an unforgettable night.

Outside, the world was beginning to wake up.

But inside the suite, time seemed to move slower.

The celebration had lasted for hours.

Music had filled the air beneath crystal chandeliers while the smooth rhythm of the jazz band carried guests from the dance floor to long conversations over candlelit tables.

Laughter echoed through the ballroom, glasses clinked together in celebration, and friends and family lingered long after the band played its final note.

No one had wanted to leave.

Because what began as a wedding had turned into
something far more powerful.

A night of joy.

A night of confrontation.

A night of forgiveness.

Somewhere between the chaos and the quiet prayers
spoken in the middle of that reception hall, the evening
had ended with a sense of closure neither Sampson nor
Elisa had expected.

Old wounds had surfaced.

But healing had stepped into the room too.

Now the morning felt calm.

Almost sacred.

Elisa stirred first, her eyes slowly adjusting to the soft golden light filtering through the curtains. For a moment she simply lay still, letting the quiet settle around her.

Her body felt tired in the best way, like someone who had finally laid down a heavy burden.

She turned slightly and smiled when she saw Sampson still asleep beside her.

His arm rested loosely across her waist, his breathing slow and even. The tension that had lived in his shoulders for so long was gone, replaced by the peaceful exhaustion of a man who had faced everything the night before.

Elisa studied his face for a moment.

"Husband," she whispered softly to herself, the word still new enough to make her laugh.

Sampson shifted beside her as if her voice had reached him even in sleep. A moment later his eyes opened slowly, adjusting to the light.

He blinked once.

Then smiled.

"Good morning, Mrs. Davis," he murmured, his voice still rough with sleep.

Elisa laughed quietly.

"Good morning, Mr. Davis."

For a moment they simply lay there, soaking in the stillness.

No cameras.

No guests.

No producers whispering instructions.

No music floating through the air.

Just the quiet reality that they had made it through everything.

Sampson stretched slightly before reaching toward the nightstand where his phone rested. The screen lit up the moment he picked it up, vibrating with a flood of overnight notifications.

Messages.

Tags.

Missed calls.

He chuckled lightly.

"Probably everyone congratulating us," he said casually.

Elisa nodded and reached for her own phone.

"I'm sure my girls have started at the group chat already," she joked.

But the moment her screen lit up…..her smile faded.

Sampson noticed instantly.

The shift in her face was small, but it was enough.

"What's wrong?" he asked, sitting up slightly.

Elisa didn't answer right away.

Her eyes remained locked on the screen.

Sampson frowned.

"Elisa?"

Slowly, she turned the phone toward him.

Across the top of the screen was a photograph taken from the reception.

Sampson instantly recognized the moment.

It was the confrontation.

Him gripping Leonard's collar.

Guests frozen in shock around them.

And above the image, bold black letters stretched across the screen.

THE PERFECT COUPLE… OR A HOT MESS EXPRESS?

Below it sat the byline.

Vira Kelly — Exclusive

Sampson closed his eyes briefly and rubbed his fingers through his beard.

"Of course," he muttered.

Sampson kept scrolling.

And with every swipe of her finger, the silence in the room grew heavier.

Vira hadn't simply covered the wedding drama.

She had investigated it.

The article unfolded like a carefully constructed storm.

Leonard's name appeared first.

Then his criminal history.

Old arrest records were displayed clearly within the article, legal documents describing the abuse Elisa had suffered as a child.

The language was clinical.

Cold.

Detached.

Every painful detail laid out for the world to read.

There was no mention of the years Elisa spent healing.

No mention of therapy.

No mention of forgiveness.

Just the crime.

Sampson's jaw tightened.

Elisa kept scrolling.

The next section shifted the spotlight.

Sampson Davis: The Complicated Past Behind the Perfect Groom

The article detailed Sampson's childhood, how his father had disappeared from his life when he was young.

The story painted the absence in harsh strokes, framing it as emotional abandonment that shaped the man he became.

Sampson exhaled slowly.

But Vira hadn't stopped there.

The article continued.

Old interviews.

Archived social media posts.

Fragments of conversations.

All pieced together to highlight the strained relationship Sampson once had with his mother.

Moments that had once been private.

Moments that had been worked through in therapy.

Moments that had healed.

Now presented as evidence of dysfunction.

Sampson leaned back against the headboard slowly.

"She really went all the way with this one," he said quietly.

Elisa didn't respond.

Her thumb continued scrolling down the screen.

The final section of the article appeared.

A bold headline read:

The Family No One Talks About

Elisa's hand froze.

Her eyes stopped moving.

Sampson noticed immediately.

"What is it?" he asked.

Elisa slowly lowered the phone.

Her voice barely rose above a whisper.

"She's not finished."

Sampson frowned.

"What do you mean?"

Elisa turned the phone back toward him.

At the very bottom of the article sat one final paragraph written in Vira's signature dramatic tone.

"While the newlyweds appear to have overcome extraordinary challenges, one major figure in Elisa Davis's life remains curiously absent from the story. Sources say little is known about Elisa's mother, we know her dad died when she was 9 years old, that raises an interesting question. Who is she… and where has she been all this time? Stay tuned as we uncover the truth."

Sampson stared at the screen.

Elisa slowly placed the phone down on the bed between them.

The peaceful quiet of the morning had vanished.

Outside, the sun continued rising as if nothing had changed.

But somewhere beyond the walls of that suite

Vira Kelly was already digging.

Searching.

Asking questions.

And if she found what she was looking for.

The wedding drama everyone had just watched would only be the beginning.

The next chapter of Sampson and Elisa story was already on its way.

The room felt different now.

Not louder.

Not quieter.

Just… heavier.

Elisa sat at the edge of the bed, her phone still resting beside her like something dangerous, something that had already done its damage but hadn't finished yet.

The sunlight still poured through the curtains.

The same soft glow.

The same peaceful morning.

But peace no longer lived in the room the way it had just moments before.

Because now the world knew.

Or at least, the world thought it did.

Elisa wrapped her arms around herself, her mind racing in ways she hadn't felt in a long time. Not since before therapy. Not since before she had found the courage to speak her truth out loud.

She had healed.

She knew she had healed.

She had done the work.

The long nights.

The tears.

The counseling sessions that forced her to revisit memories she once buried so deeply she thought they'd never resurface.

She had forgiven.

Not just Leonard—but the past itself.

She had found God in the middle of her brokenness.

Found peace in places she once only felt pain.

And yet—

here it was again.

Not the trauma itself.

But the exposure of it.

Laid out for strangers.

Consumed by people who didn't know her.

Didn't love her.

Didn't care about her healing.

Elisa shook her head slowly, almost in disbelief.

"I just…" she whispered, her voice trembling slightly, "I don't understand how someone can be that heartless."

Sampson stood near the window, his back partially turned, his jaw tight as he stared out at the quiet world below.

"People like that," he said quietly, "don't see people."

He turned toward her.

"They see stories. Headlines. Opportunities."

Elisa exhaled slowly.

Her eyes dropped to the floor.

"I've always been careful," she said. "Always private. Always guarded."

Sampson walked closer, listening.

"My motto has always been… the less people know about you, the less they can hold over your head."

Her voice cracked slightly.

"And now…" she gestured toward the phone, "…the whole world has access."

Sampson's fists clenched at his sides.

That was the part he couldn't shake.

Not the headlines about him.

Not the pieces about his father.

Not even the way Vira had twisted his relationship with his mother into something it wasn't anymore.

He could take that.

He would take that.

But Elisa?

Her innocence.

Her pain.

Her story.

That was never supposed to belong to the world.

Sampson running his fingers through his beard, frustration building in his chest.

"I should've stopped this," he muttered.

Elisa looked up.

"Samspon….."

"I should've protected you," he said, his voice heavier now. "From all of this."

"You can't control people like her," Elisa said gently.

"But I'm your husband," he shot back, emotion rising. "That's my job."

The words hung in the air.

Not harsh.

Not angry.

Just honest.

Sampson turned away again, pacing slowly now.

"I don't care what she says about me," he continued. "She can dig up whatever she wants about my dad… my mom… my past."

He shook his head.

"That's nothing."

He stopped walking.

"But this?" he said, turning back to her. "What she did to you?"

His voice dropped.

"That's different."

Elisa watched him carefully.

This wasn't just anger.

It was something deeper.

Helplessness.

Sampson exhaled sharply.

"How do I protect you from something like that?" he asked. "How do I stop the world from taking what you went through and turning it into… content?"

Elisa didn't answer right away.

Because she didn't have a simple answer.

Instead, she stood slowly and walked toward him.

"Sampson," she said softly.

He looked at her.

"We've already been through the worst," she continued. "We faced it. We healed from it. We didn't run from it."

She placed her hand over his.

"That doesn't change just because people are talking."

Sampson looked down at her hand, then back at her.

"But trials don't stop just because you've healed," Elisa said quietly.

Her voice carried a calm strength now.

"You can heal. You can grow. You can forgive. You can find God…"

She paused.

"But trials will come."

Sampson's expression shifted slightly.

"And the enemy?" she continued. "He's always going to find ways to test your faith."

The words settled deep between them.

Not as fear.

But as truth.

Sampson nodded slowly.

He understood that.

He had lived that.

But understanding it didn't make it easier.

Elisa stepped closer.

"We don't fight this the way the world fights," she said. "We don't respond with chaos."

Sampson looked at her, searching.

"Then what do we do?" he asked.

Elisa took a slow breath.

Her eyes drifted briefly toward the phone on the bed.

Then back to him.

"We stand," she said simply.

Sampson studied her face.

Strong.

Grounded.

Unshaken, even now.

And yet—

He knew this wasn't over.

Not even close.

Because somewhere out there—

Vira Kelly was still digging.

Still searching.

Still pulling at threads that Elisa herself had never fully unraveled.

Sampson's jaw tightened again.

Because this time, it wasn't just about what had already been exposed.

It was about what was coming next.

He glanced toward the phone again.

Toward the article.

Toward the final line that lingered like a warning.

Elisa's mother.

A story neither of them had spoken about.

A past neither of them had fully explored.

Sampson turned back to Elisa.

His voice quieter now.

More focused.

"I don't know what she's going to find," he said.

Elisa didn't respond.

Because deep down….. she wasn't sure either.

Sampson took a slow breath.

But one thing was certain.

"I'm going to protect you," he said firmly.

"Whatever it takes."

Elisa held his gaze.

And for the first time since reading the article. There was a flicker of uncertainty in her eyes.

Because healing had brought them this far.

But this?

This felt like the beginning of something else.

Something deeper.

Something hidden.

And somewhere in the distance

a truth was waiting to be uncovered.

One that might test everything they thought they had already overcome.

She felt the confirmation in Sampson's voice as he stated he would protect her at all costs.

And she there was nothing she could say in that moment to prevent him from doing exactly that.

Acknowledgments

First and foremost, I give all honor and glory to God for changing my heart. A Tarina centered in Christ has been a beautiful thing, and with Him I know I am unstoppable. His grace, patience, and guidance have shaped my journey and given me the strength to complete this book.

I thank my mother, **Theresa Robinson**, for her constant encouragement and support as I worked to finish this book. Your belief in me reminded me that what God placed in my heart was worth completing. Your sacrifices helped me get here, and I am forever grateful.

To my dad, **Otis Driver Sr.**, thank you for always making me feel like your little girl from the day I was born. You have always been my protector, loving me unconditionally and reminding me what it truly means to be loved and protected.

To my dad, **Anderson Brown Jr.**, thank you for being open, honest, and transparent with me. That alone has allowed our relationship to blossom into something truly beautiful. I never have to question where I stand in your life, you make it known and felt. Our relationship is a true testament to healing, love, and elevation, and I am incredibly thankful for the bond we have today.

Now to the life I created—**Marc, Kee**, and **Kaylin**. You three have helped shape the woman I am today. You pushed me to grow, expanded my capacity to love, and gave my life a deeper sense of purpose. I love you more than words could ever express.

Saving the best for last to my husband **Larry Tolbert Jr.** Thank you for sharing me with this book. There were many long days, and countless hours spent writing at Barnes & Noble. You never questioned it, instead, you understood and encouraged me to see it through. Your support meant everything. Thank you for your love, for the extra push, and most importantly, for believing in me. Always #TeamTolbert

This is only the beginning of what God has* for me on this journey of writing. And to everyone who has supported me along the way, through encouragement, prayer, or simply believing in me—**THANK YOU!**

* AI was used for editing purposes only.

ABOUT THE AUTHOR

Tarina Michelle' is a wife, mother, writer, pastor, poet at heart, and world-changer whose pen was sharpened early on. From writing and selling poems in middle school for Valentine's Day and in high school rapping and crafting stories pulled from real life situations. Words became her weapon, her therapy, and ultimately her calling.

She is not one thing; she is too many things to be contained. Tarina Michelle' writes urban fiction layered with biblical truth, blending real life realities with spiritual depth; never preachy, never forced. Her stories hit hard, love deep, and move honestly, speaking to broken places while pointing toward healing. She doesn't belt faith over your head, yet she weaves it through the struggle, the grind, and the growth.

Unapologetically creative and purpose-driven, Tarina Michelle' shares her gifts with the world through bold storytelling that challenges limits and awakens destiny. She writes for the misunderstood, those who are growing in their faith, and the rising, reminding readers that no matter where you start, redemption is real, purpose is waiting, and you were built to change the world.

Why Didn't You Save me is her debut novel.

More from Tarina-Michelle

Coming Soon

"The Destined Duo"

A continuation of Elisa and Sampson's journey.